The Doll Maker

Claire Highton-Stevenson

ISBN: 9781790206803
ISBN-13: 9781790206803

This is a work of fiction. Names, characters, businesses, places, events, locales, and incidents are either the products of the author's imagination or used in a fictitious manner. Any resemblance to actual persons, living or dead, or actual events is purely coincidental.

DEDICATION

For all the men and women, in and out of uniform, who step up in our
time of need.

ACKNOWLEDGMENTS

Michelle Arnold
Dean Jones BA (ed) hons MSc Dr Crimj
Senior Forensic Pathology Manager
May Dawney
PC Rick Flynn
Without whom this book would not have moved any further than my imagination.

Prologue

He hadn't grown up *knowing* that he would murder another person, let alone several, but he had. Hadn't everybody considered doing it? Only he had actually done it, and now it was all that consumed him. The small voice in his head grew louder with every passing day, soothing his worries, whispering encouragement and prodding him forwards.

It wasn't as grisly as the movies made out. There was blood, of course, but it hadn't been the stomach-curdling event that he thought it would be. Blind rage would do that for you. Or maybe he was just different, unaffected.

Thinking back to the moment when it first came down to it, he knew it was meant to be. He understood that as he took in the artistry of his creation, but it wasn't quite right. He was still working on that part. Funny, how it had just come to him like that. Just a flicker of a memory and he had the perfect accessory.

It was 9:04. A.M. when it happened; he knew that because he had looked at his watch just seconds before she had started. He just wanted to read the newspaper, but her voice shrieking across the room like a drunken banshee had grated on him. It went through him like nails down a chalkboard. He cocked his head at her, and right then, in that precise moment, he knew he would kill her. He knew it like he knew the sky was blue and grass was green. It was that simple.

In the background he could hear the faint echoes of a Whitney Houston song playing on the radio. Remnants of snow lingered outside through the cracked window pane. Winter had come late this year. He felt the hard, wooden floor beneath his feet, threadbare carpets doing little to cushion his steps. When he looked at her again, it wasn't *her* face that gawped back at him, reminding him why it was that she preferred his absence. She had friends coming over; she didn't want him hanging around tonight. The same excuses. It used to be because he was too young; now it was because he was too old.

He moved with such speed that she didn't even register the change in him. Too busy with her own selfish need to enjoy the pleasures in life to be concerned with him, and that was when he knew why he would kill her: because she reminded him of her. His mother.

His fist was first to react. A direct hit between the eyes, smashing the bridge of her nose in a bone-crunching blow. She staggered, but the bitch held firm, numb from the booze and drugs that consumed her. Her expression at first was quizzical when he grabbed her by the throat. As he began to squeeze, then she knew. He saw the fear within her. Her eyes bulging, his grip tightening.

"It's all your fault," he hissed, spittle bathing her face as he pulled her closer to him. "You and your filthy, vile and disgusting lifestyle-" His grip loosened a little. He would take his time. Anger was pushing him onwards, but hate would make this worthwhile.

"-without you and him," he snarled at the thought of his father. "Without you both, she would still be here."

"Please, baby don't. Come on, I'll do anything." Her voice was scratchy as she gasped for every breath, to no avail. He remembered pleading similarly as a child not to be sent away; to no avail either. "Anything you want," she tugged at her top, showing him her tits; he liked her tits. He let go of her throat then and for a second she thought maybe, it would be okay. Until he slapped her. His palm hard against her cheek.

"You made her do it." His fingers wrapped around her scrawny neck once more. She had no idea what he was talking about as she clawed at his arms. His face contorted with a mix of rage and sadness, his eyes brimming with tears. "Because of you, she did it," he half-whispered, half-sobbed as his fingers gripped tighter.

The blackness came for her, as she knew it would. Her entire life she had lived with the blackness, the dark side of existence engulfing her before she had even had a chance at life. She had never thought it would come from someone like him though. He had adored her, fucked her because he wanted to, not because he was paying, though there were times he had paid for something more 'special.' There were many times under a man that she considered how her life would end. While they paid to thrust into her, she would take her mind elsewhere. Her thoughts would start off light: the idea of escaping it all, the addictions and the lifestyle that came with them, but eventually her thoughts would move towards the end. Her death would be lonely. Forgotten easily.

Afterwards, when he was finished with her, when she was displayed just the way he wanted her, he set about finishing the work.

The doll would be a reminder when they eventually found her.

Chapter One

Dark grey clouds comforted the sky on a harsh November night. The moonlight was barely visible. It had rained earlier, and the grass was now sodden and waterlogged in places, the beginnings of a frost. With the weather as bad as it had been lately, this area should have been desolate, nothing more than the tiny creatures that lived among the bramble and trees, not like now, with the noisy generator that was working the overhead lamps. The bright white forensic tent, that was hurriedly erected the minute the CSM got here, stood out like a sore thumb. Onlookers gawped out from beneath umbrellas and raincoats at the macabre scene now hidden from them.

Home office pathologist Dr Tristan Barnard was virtually unrecognisable in his all-in-one white forensic jumpsuit. In amongst his team of scientific evidence collectors, they looked like pins in a bowling alley that had been scattered. Some were lying prostrate on the floor, examining God knows what in fingertip searches. Others were standing around talking in quiet voices, filling in forms and waiting for further instructions.

Detective Inspector Sophie Whitton stood silently on the periphery, watching like a hawk. Her tall and wiry frame stood stoically as she glanced around the cordoned-off area. It was how she always surveyed the scene: standing back from it, taking it all in. Inquisitive eyes looked out from under a mop of black hair that hung longer at the front than the back. She swept a hand through it and felt the damp air slowly soaking in, before shoving her hands into her pockets. Hunching her shoulders against the cold, she blew a puff of hot air out.

The basic questions. Why here? Is there something special about the place that links to the killer, or the victim? How did he, or she, get the body here? Was the victim already dead, and this is just the body dump site? Or is this the execution site too? She went through everything in her head and drew her conclusions. Only later would she start to dissect them and focus on the areas that she could find answers for.

After pulling on her own forensic booties to match, she followed the designated pathway that forensics had deemed clear to walk on without fucking up the crime scene, until she found herself at the doorway to the tent. Chief Inspector Adam Turner stood hunched over the body like an old man taking a rest.

"House to house is taking place right now," he informed his detective. She nodded. She already knew that would be the case; it was standard practice. He turned to leave. "I'll see you back at the station."

Tristan was bent down on one knee examining what Sophie knew to be the body of a young woman. There was nothing unusual in that; women turned up dead on her patch as often as young men did. No, what was unusual was what had been done to this body.

A dog walker had called it in. Out for a late Sunday afternoon stroll with her spaniel, Daisy, Mrs Florence Marchant had the unfortunate occasion to come across the partially decomposing corpse. She usually took an alternative route but the pathway had been flooded, so they had taken a different path and ended up here. Otherwise, it could have been days before they found her.

"Estimation on the time of death to be around 48 hours ago," Tristan's well-spoken voice said as he turned briefly to acknowledge the Detective's presence. "Asphyxia by manual strangulation would be my best guess right now. We're quite some way from full on putrefaction, but that's more likely to be the colder weather than the time that's holding it off. Let's all be thankful it isn't June. Slight bloating to the neck and abdomen, what's left of it anyway." He stood up, towering above everybody else. "We've got animal interference. Or a cannibal." He chuckled at his little joke. Whitton didn't smile. "Anyway, the incision site has attracted attention from the local habitat." He coughed and cleared his throat. "The spleen is missing."

"Did he leave one?" She asked the question, but wasn't sure she wanted the answer. It had been almost three months since the last, and eight since the first.

Knowing exactly what she was asking, Tristan shook his head. "If he did, it wasn't found with the body this time."

"So it might not be him then?" Her voice was unusually hopeful, until the Doc shook his head slowly. "The missing spleen could just be the animal interference?"

"No, it might not be, but...it fits." She tilted her head and waited for the explanation. "It would be highly unusual that an animal hit pot luck and chewed the exact spot that the spleen can be found. Plus, there is the additional post mortem modification. But there is no doll this time...or at least, we haven't found one."

"That's going to piss him off then," she said, her lips pressed together in a firm line, her jaw twitching in frustration. "But, if we're lucky, then this is it, his spree is done?"

"We can always hope for that. The surrounding area is being scoured as we speak I believe. If he left one then the team will find it." He spoke quietly as he passed his clipboard to a colleague. His grey eyes softened as he waited for her next question.

"Do we have any ID yet?" Her voice was quiet, and she waited while he pulled off his latex gloves with a snap and tossed them into the receptacle on the floor.

"No, not yet, but if she's in the system then I should have it by morning. Otherwise it's a case of dental records, and hoping that someone is missing her." Whitton moved closer to the body. She had seen plenty of corpses in her time: fifteen years on the job, the last four in C.I.D. It didn't faze her anymore, at least not when they were first found. When they were just a body, and didn't have a name or a family.

The victim was young, mid-thirties. Her hair had been blonde once, now just a muddied nest of tangles. She had been posed on her back in a macabre image of Sleeping Beauty. Her eyes had been removed though. Decomposition was beginning to set in.

Her clothes had been piled neatly next to her, blue jeans and a black top with green trainers. It reminded Whitton of a bruise. Whoever she was had been re-dressed in pyjamas. Light blue silk with beautiful ivory buttons that looked expensive. Just like the others.

She rubbed her hand over her face and grimaced. "This is the third one, and we're still no closer to catching the bastard." She spoke with no malice. It wasn't the forensic team's fault. Every scrap of evidence there was to be had, they had found and processed; it just hadn't led anywhere. She wasn't ruling anything out at this stage, but this killer, or these killers, were smart.

"You know eventually they will slip up, and when they-"

"Yeah, yeah...when they do we will catch them. I know. Doesn't bring any comfort to the family of this one, or the two before it though, does it?" She was weary. Eight months, and all they had was a psych evaluation to go on, some creepy dolls, and the fact that he liked to dress them in pyjamas. She checked her watch: 9:30 p.m. "I'm going to head back, you'll-"

"I'll let you know, yes, soon as we have something."

It was raining again now as she stepped outside of the tent, that fine drizzle that seemed to seep into your bones and freeze your very core. The techs worked in relative silence, painstakingly logging every blade of grass that might hold even the minutest of clues. The tinny sound of her phone ringing broke the silence and she made an urgent grab for it, pushing past the small collection of press all waiting for that confirmation so they could get the by-line written before the night's deadline.

"Whitton."

"Soph, its Dale." Her partner for this case sounded cold as his voice echoed through the airways. For a brief second she thought it might have been Yvonne, apologising for the way she had left things when Sophie had had to leave half way through dinner, but she knew that wouldn't happen. Firstly, Yvonne didn't back down if she thought she was right, and secondly, she knew not to interrupt when Sophie was on a call out like this. Dale's voice brought her back from her thoughts. "We found it."

"Where?" She began moving quickly down the path back towards her car.

"Copers Field." He was walking too, she could tell by his breathing. "She's blonde right, like the others? Doc's theory of the Three Wise Monkeys looks more promising with this one's eyes...ya know?"

"Yeah." She yanked off the white forensic booties and balled them up, ready to throw in the bin provided. She stopped then to listen to him properly. The wind was picking up, and he sounded a little muffled as he cupped the handset to speak.

"Laid out like the others?" She tucked her phone between her ear and shoulder, as she lit up and took a drag on the cigarette.

"Yeah, on her back, redressed in silk pyjamas." Her hand subconsciously raked through her short, dark hair. Dale sucked in a breath against her ear.

"So, it's him then. Poor cow," he almost whispered. He was looking at the doll, knowing that whatever injury had been inflicted on it, would be the same for the victim.

"Yeah, it's him. I'll meet you back at the station."

Chapter Two

The Criminal Investigation Department (C.I.D) was never closed. There always seemed to be somebody sitting at a desk working a case. Tonight was no different, as Detectives Whitton and Saint pored over the files from the two previous bodies.

"Let's go over them again." Sophie sighed. She rubbed at her face, the strip lighting overhead doing nothing to ease the nagging headache that was building behind her eyes. Raising her arm, she checked her watch. Midnight already. Another late night; another argument with Yvonne, most likely.

The relationship was on the wane, but neither seemed in a hurry to end it. Instead they continued on in a silent acknowledgement. If nobody said it out loud, then all was fine. Until Sophie's job got in the way; a recurring issue it seemed.

Detective Sergeant Dale Saint threw his head back and pointed out the obvious. "We've *been* over them. Nothing has changed."

"Maybe we missed something. It won't hurt to go over it again," she challenged him. His blue eyes, watery with exhaustion, stared back at her, incredulous.

"For fuck's sake Sophie," he huffed. He was frustrated. They both were. Everybody wanted this maniac off of the streets as soon as possible. He blew out a breath before opening the folder and reading from the page. "Anjelika Tyszka was the first. Thirty-three-year-old Polish national, in the UK to work and study. Was supposed to meet friends in a local bar at approximately 7 p.m., the same bar she worked part time in. She didn't make it."

"Which friends was she meeting?" She stood now, pacing the small area around their desk and the murder board. Dale scanned the page with his finger.

"A...Tanya Jones and...Beth Pritchard. Both were spoken to, and both said they didn't know anything. Anjelika didn't turn up, and they just assumed she had changed her mind."

"The doll was found with her, posed in the same sleeping position next to her, and with its mouth sewn shut?" She stopped pacing, her mind whirring as she moved toward Dale and read the file over his shoulder. "Clothes piled neatly like this one, and redressed in pink silk pyjamas?"

"Yeah, with the incision site for the spleen left open, and the spleen removed from the body." He shuddered at the memory.

"Because she was at home, he had time, wasn't going to be disturbed. Same tonight. It's a field in the middle of nowhere - pretty much nobody goes there at this time of year. He had time to undress her, fold the clothes and torture her, but with the second victim..." She reached across for the file. "Emma Taylor, she was supposed to be at work in the local pub, right?"

"Yeah, she arrived just before her shift started, but never actually appeared behind the bar. The landlady found her thirty minutes later."

"The doll was there, but she was still dressed." She pushed both hands through her hair. "He planned to redress her, he had green pyjamas this time, but he didn't. Why?"

"I dunno. He still managed to cut off her ears and cut her open." He screwed his face up at the memory of Emma Taylor. The papers were asking if this was a new Ripper.

"But he didn't take the spleen from Emma."

Saint stood up and looked at the map on the board. Three pink pins marked the spot where the bodies had been found. He picked up some string and tied it around the pin that marked Anjelika's body, then he linked it to the pin that held the location of Emma Taylor's body before lastly tying it to the newest pin to mark the board. Whitton watched. "Ainsley Road, that's where Anjelika lived and the doll was found." He poked at the pin. "Emma Taylor worked at the White Bull on Stanford St." Another poke of the pin. "But the as-yet-unidentified female's doll was discovered at Copers Field."

"Fuck." She had thought for moment that he was onto something. Deflated, she slumped back in her chair and let her head fall back.

Frustrated, he walked back across the room to his desk, picked up his coffee and took a mouthful, wincing when he realised it was stone cold. "So why place the doll away from the body this time?"

"It doesn't make sense. He has a pattern, why deviate again?" Whitton growled her annoyance. Dale sat at his desk, his unshaven face resting on a palm, just staring at her. Her phone buzzed, the screen lighting up with Yvonne's name. "Let's call it a day." She sighed, stifling a yawn in the process. The tiredness was soaking into her bones, soaking into her life, through every growing crack in her psyche.

Chapter Three

One drink led to another; it always had. Nicolas could barely remember a time when it hadn't. It wasn't his fault; just one of those things. Something in the genes, he supposed during times when he was sober enough to try and work it out.

He had never hidden it. In the beginning it had been attractive to her. He was the party king, dressed to the nines in designer jeans and shirts that cost more money than most earned during the week. He would strut his stuff on the dancefloors of every club London had to offer. And he would drink. Champagne, tequila, any and every cocktail; and at the end of the night he would chase it all down with scotch or brandy. Lately, though, it was vodka. It didn't matter with vodka. If he bought the cheaper brands, it all washed down the same way, unlike scotch; you needed a decent scotch to really enjoy it. Stretching his meagre savings to afford such a delicacy was a little silly when he could buy vodka for half the price.

Every weekend he would head into town and blow handfuls of cash entertaining the ladies. Of course, eventually one lady had stood out from the pack. Georgie was wonderful, the kind of woman you took home to your parents. She had an aura about her, something so innate that it took his breath away whenever he was within a foot of her. A redhead, beautiful. Tall and slender, dance moves to match, and she was just as 'up for it' as he had been. So, he married her.

Those first years together were bliss. They continued on with the lifestyle they loved, partying until the small hours. They were the couple that everybody envied. He watched as men, and the odd woman, all tried to pry her attention from him, but she never looked elsewhere. She adored him, was besotted, and would do anything for him, and he for her. Their life revolved around enjoying the club scene and all that came with it. Their friends were just like them too. It was just how everybody was back then, only they all grew up and out of it, and he didn't. For him it was just another day, day after day of fun, and fun meant drinking and partying.

Until the day that she announced she was pregnant.

Pregnancy was not something either of them had planned, not right then at least, but she looked so happy about it. Of course, they were still kids themselves - kids with too much money, too much time, and not enough reality.

Nothing much changed. They got a nanny, and Tiffany was well looked after. For ten years, everything was perfect as far as he was concerned. The child rarely complained and Georgie, well she just blossomed.

But, one night of exuberance and a broken condom had meant another pregnancy. Reality bit hard. He had tried to pressure her into getting rid of it, but she wouldn't hear of it. Something had changed; *she* had changed. No longer wanting to go out drinking and dancing, she wanted a family. Still, it didn't stop him from doing as he pleased. At first they argued about it, but then she just seemed to accept it and they fell into a routine.

Tiffany became a difficult child, especially after the accident. She wanted attention, and went off the rails in order to get it. With the baby taking up all of Georgie's time, she became disobedient. By the time she was 15 she had already run away three times, been brought home by the police for drinking under age, and attempted to kill herself.

He realised now, as he sat alone in his room, that maybe they could have done things differently with their daughter. They didn't make the same mistakes with the baby. As soon as he was of age, he was sent to boarding school. Georgie had been upset at first, wanting to have the relationship with this child that she had missed out on with Tiffany. And then with the loss of Tiffany, his wife had hit the doldrums.

But, he had picked his wife well. She wouldn't leave him; she would evolve back into the woman he fell in love with. He loved them all in his own way, but he loved the drink more. It consumed him then, and continued to now.

As he sat in his chair, alone in a room nobody visited, he wondered if things really could have been different. But as he lifted the bottle and poured the clear liquid over the cubes of ice, he knew that there had never been a different path for him.

His wife has gone now. Loyally, she had stayed, but an accident had meant she was taken from him. He missed her; she was his conscience, his saviour.

Life would be lonely with just his booze for company. Karma was an ironic bitch.

Chapter Four

The flat was in complete darkness when Whitton finally fell through the door. Exhaustion from the long hours of the day, and the added stress a case always brought with it, tugged at her itchy, tired eyes. She shrugged off her coat and hung it on the rack, grateful for the central heating and Yvonne's insistence that their living space should be on a par with the Bahamas.

She was hungry, but the thought of actually eating anything right now just brought with it a nauseous feeling. She couldn't shake the image of the latest victim. This one, she felt, was worse than the others for some reason. She was just hoping that, like the others, she was already dead when he went to work on gouging her eyes out, and removing her spleen.

Flicking the tiny torch on her phone to on, she made her way quietly through the flat and into the bedroom. Yvonne was already asleep, curled up on her side of the bed, cocooned beneath the duvet. For a moment, Sophie considered sleeping on the couch so as not to bother her, but her bed was comfortable, and she needed to sleep deeply. The thought of Yvonne waking, however, and having to actually have a conversation with her right now, was just something she really didn't want to deal with. Blowing out a breath, she began stripping off her work clothes, reasoning that being found on the couch would warrant a bigger conversation, another one she wasn't ready to have just yet.

The sheets were cool on her side, and she felt a light shiver as she climbed into bed and pulled the heavy cover up and over her.

She would normally have put on pyjamas, but that would involve opening and closing drawers, so she went without. The room was illuminated a little by the red digits on the alarm clock Yvonne used. She would be up in a little over five hours, off to the office to number crunch for another day. Sophie often wondered how she did it, the same thing over and over for five days, 9-5, Monday till Friday. It would drive Sophie to distraction. She needed the unpredictability, the randomness her job as a copper gave her. Yvonne hated it, wanted her to pack it all in and get a job for some private security firm, sitting behind a desk.

"What time is it?" Yvonne murmured, her voice full of sleep.

"Time you were asleep," Sophie whispered back.

"Hmm, I'd sleep better knowing where you were." She leaned up a little and squinted, heavy-lidded, at the clock. "Jesus Soph, it's past midnight, again." She flopped back against the pillow as Sophie sighed.

"We found another body." Her voice was flat. It wasn't an excuse, it was a *reason,* and she needed Yvonne to understand that. "It was bad. Worse this time than the last." She stared up into the darkness, at the ceiling she knew was there just feet above her head. "I'm worried we won't catch him."

Yvonne remained silent, and Sophie assumed she had probably fallen back to sleep until she said, "Maybe you should let someone else do it." *That* was her response. Let someone else deal with this evil. Let someone else find the killer. Let it be someone else. Anyone else but you.

"It's my job, Von. Why can't you just accept that? Support me?" Sophie argued, banging her back into the pillows.

"I do-"

"No, you don't. I'm a copper Vonnie, this is what I do, and I'm good at it. It's what I've always done." Sophie grabbed her pillow and got up. "I'll sleep on the couch."

~Doll~

As 5 a.m. tick-tocked on the mantle clock, she gave up trying to sleep and got up. Dressing in clean underwear and yesterday's clothes, she was out of the door before Yvonne was even awake. That was happening a lot lately. Arguments had become the norm. Grumbling at each other over everything and nothing, and avoidance was how they had been dealing with it. She knew it wasn't particularly mature, and that she would need to address it soon, but right now wasn't the time. She needed to focus on this case and bring these women some justice.

Lying in the dark, her mind had gone over and over the details of the case. Something was nagging at her, but she couldn't put her finger on it. She needed the files.

When she pulled into the station's carpark, she spotted Dale climbing out of his own vehicle. "What you doing here so early?"

she called out across the yard. Cupping her hand around the lighter, protecting against the wind, she lit a cigarette and inhaled.

"Could say the same about you. Got a spare?" he said as he approached. She pulled out the pack from her top pocket and tossed it at him. His blonde hair was darker now, still wet from a shower. His clothes were fresh, Becky obviously making sure he was presentable before he left.

"Thought you'd given up." She smiled as he lit the fag and tossed the box back at her. She caught it one-handed and shoved it back inside her top pocket.

"I have. So, why you here so early?" he asked, inhaling deeply before blowing a long stream of smoke up into the air.

"Couldn't sleep, something's-"

"Nagging? Yeah, I've got the same feeling. Beck's kicked me out before I woke up the girls with my constant pacing." She chuckled at that image. Rebecca Hanson was not a woman to be messed with when it came to her kids being tired and therefore grumpy all day.

~Doll~

The office was quiet. Jeff Branson was in, but he had beaten a hasty retreat and headed down to the cafeteria for breakfast the minute Andy Bowen had walked through the door. They were working a case together too, money laundering and dead gangsters, but it was wrapping up, and Whitton was going to nab them for her case. Both of them were good cops and would be invaluable to her.

Nothing had changed overnight. The files were where they had left them, half scattered across Sophie's desk along with photographs of the crime scenes and empty chocolate bar wrappers, the other half piled neatly. Dale Saint flopped into his chair and raised his feet up onto the desk, hands behind his head as he stared at the murder board. Sophie did the same from where she had perched on the corner of her desk. The pair of them hoping that something would jump out at them and give them the lead they needed.

"We're missing something," she stated simply as she looked back down at her desk, at the files. One caught her eye: Emma Taylor, the second victim. She reached out and picked it up, flicked it open and re-read it.

"Anything from Barnard yet?" Dale asked.

"Nope. I doubt we will get anything before ten." She moved a sheet of paper and continued to read, flicking between incident reports. "They're all blonde, green eyes, similar height and build...Emma Taylor..."

"Yeah? Second victim," he replied.

"Yeah, fully clothed." She looked up at him from the file and considered that.

"Well yeah, she wasn't naked, but you could hardly suggest she was fully clothed. The way he had her displayed...*everything* was uncovered."

Sophie smiled humorously. Her partner's inability to say what he saw when it came to a naked woman intrigued her. How he had managed to land Becky and have two kids, she would never know.

"All strangled, and then dissected post-mortem," she continued.

Emma had been placed sitting upright against the wall. Her skirt had been hiked up, and her underwear yanked down. Her t-shirt, the uniform one all the staff wore, was pulled upwards along with her bra to reveal her breasts. Strangled, just like the others, and he had cut her ears off.

"What if the reason she wasn't changed into the pyjamas was because he was disturbed? What if something spooked him when he was trying to change her clothes?"

"But, what? Nobody at the pub admits to coming out there in the time frame. The back gate leads out into an empty alley," Dale countered. He wasn't against the idea. On the contrary, he agreed, but they liked to play this game. One came up with a scenario, and the other would try and bat it away with the reasons why it wasn't possible. It helped to weed out the impossibilities and leave them with just the probables.

"It doesn't make sense that he spends all that time on Vic One undressing her and posing her, dissecting her, and then he does the same with Vic Three. So, it's his preferred choice!" she emphasised. "And if he had the opportunity with Vic Two then he would have done the same because he left the pyjamas, but he didn't, and there has to be a reason for that, that didn't fit with him and his motives."

"So, let's go back down there and take a look," he answered, grabbing his jacket from the back of his chair.

Chapter Five

The White Bull Public House was built in 1705 according to the stone carving above the door. Its mock Tudor half-timbering and whitewash meant that it stood out from the rest of the buildings that made up Stanford St. The buildings either side of it were relatively new; 1950s rebuilds. This area had taken a direct hit when Hitler's Luftwaffe were dropping their bombs and two had landed right here on Stanford St – one either side of the pub. They rebuilt the right side, but the left had become an alleyway that allowed for access to the pub and the buildings behind it.

Saint and Whitton entered the building through the saloon door and walked straight up to the bar. It was too early for the regulars holding up the bar to be in attendance. The girl restocking the shelves recognised them though and scowled.

"You caught the bastard or what?" she virtually snarled. She could have been a pretty girl if she just loosened up the tightly held ponytail on her head that had given her a somewhat startled facelift. Her make-up was over the top and tarty in Whitton's opinion too. She wore the same uniform t-shirt that Emma had worn, but had altered it by trimming the sleeves and cutting a piece out of the neckline. More flesh than necessary was flaunted and on display. The low cut of her jeans sitting on her hips showed off a red ribbon tattoo that looked out of place too. She was no gift spoiling to be opened, not with the scowl she wore so well.

"No. Need to take another look out back," Whitton responded in the only way she knew how when faced with people like this:

blunt and to the point. She didn't have time or the inclination to discuss anything with this woman and her attitude. Whitton had enough attitude of her own; she didn't need this shit on top.

They all called it the back; back yard; back alley, but in reality it was the side of the building. She was already lifting the part of the bar that allowed access through when the woman replied.

"If ya like. It's all been cleaned now though. All the blood and that's gone init."

Sophie nodded, ignoring her as she moved on through regardless. Passing through the door marked 'staff only,' they walked the long, narrow passageway that led out to the back room, a glorified staff room full of old armchairs that had seen better days. A battered old coffee table that might have actually been around in 1705 took pride of place in the centre of the room, piled high with dirty mugs and pint glasses. An ashtray that hadn't been emptied in days flowed over, and at least two cigarettes had burnt a mark on the table-top.

There were two doors: one to the left led down to the basement, a dark, dank room with no other entry points. She knew that because she had been the one that had had to go down to check it out on the night they found Emma Taylor's body.

The door they wanted was the one on the right, the only exit from the building into the small yard. No bigger than 15 feet long and with walls on three sides, it was an intimidating space. The side wall that bordered the alleyway was a solid wooden fence. A small gate to the left side of it was how the killer got in and out, they had surmised.

"So, this is where Emma was found," Dale said, pointing to the spot where the body had lain. "There was nobody in the staff room at the time, so that can't be the thing that spooked him."

"And there are no other windows on this side of the building that can look down into the yard," Sophie added. "So, what does that leave us?" They both looked around and then at each other. "The alley?"

The alleyway was a dead end. Only two other buildings had access points to it. The pub was the only one with an unlocked gate, for deliveries. It was wide enough for a van to reverse into, but you could park no more than four cars in its length. There were no street lamps other than the one on the corner where the alley met Stanford Street, so it would be dark at night.

"Maybe his plan was to bring her out here?" Sophie asked, turning around; looking for anything that would give them a lead.

"So, he kills her in the yard, or at the very least renders her unconscious and plans to bring the body here where he will be less likely to be seen, can take his time with her, but something stops him...something happens that means he must do his business in the yard, but then what? He panics and runs anyway?"

"What if we've got a witness?" Dale turned towards her voice, almost giving himself whiplash. His heart thumped at the thought.

"What if he was disturbed because someone else was out here. What if they saw him leave?" Whitton continued.

"Shit. But, how we gonna find them?"

~Doll~

Anyone visiting the morgue for the first time would probably be in for a surprise. It wasn't the sterile, cold and dark place that movies and TV cop shows would have you believe. It was a state-of-the-art complex that enabled the forensic pathologists to examine every aspect of the body and other evidence collected.

Dr Tristan Barnard was already gowned and prepped, waiting for them before he started the full autopsy. After hellos and a brief rundown of the tests, which so far had come back negative for anything untoward in the blood, he flicked the switch to his microphone and proceeded.

"The victim is a female between 30-40 years of age. She weighs 57 kilograms and is 5 feet, 4 inches tall. Evidence of trauma to the ocular area; the eyes have been gauged from the orbit post-mortem, with what I would assume to be something smooth and rounded...a spoon maybe?"

Whitton grimaced. She always felt a little odd at autopsies. Not because they were particularly nasty – she had gotten used to that part of it a long time ago – but in the way that she found the doctor's voice to be so soothing. He was describing the brutal wounds of a young and helpless woman, and yet Sophie could listen to him speak for hours. His voice was deep and calming. He would have made a wonderful storyteller.

Dale, on the other hand, had never gotten used to them. She could see him fidgeting on the periphery of her vision.

"Cutaneous bruising around the neck along with a fracture to the larynx and hyoid bone suggest manual strangulation. The assailant is right-handed." Dr Barnard paused and examined an area of skin around the abdomen. "Some animal interference around the abdominal area, jagged bite marks consistent with a canine of some sort. I'll know more once we measure and test the area, but my best guess would be a fox or stray dog." He looked up and right at Sophie as he spoke. "But, there is something else...I found lacrimal fluid on her abdomen. He appears to have cried over her." Whitton nodded an acknowledgment and jotted down the information. "Other than that, the body appears to be in a good condition. I would say that she was physically fit and healthy. Now, young Dale." He smirked behind his mask as he raised the bone saw. "Are we staying for the rest of the autopsy?"

They both knew there was more work to do for the pathologist and his team, but neither of them needed to be there to witness it. The doc would inform them if he found anything further that was unusual or pertinent to the case. So, Whitton wasn't going to make Dale Saint sit through it.

"Oh, Detectives?" Dr Barnard called out as they were just about to leave the room. "I have had a look at the doll. Our furry friend here," he nodded his head towards the victim's torso, "may have had something to do with why the doll wasn't with the body. I found canine teeth marks in it."

Chapter Six

The pathology unit for Woodington was based on the grounds of Woodington University Hospital, a newly opened building that stood proudly in its acres of freshly concreted parking.

"Is Becky working today?" Whitton asked as they cut through the hospital; it was the quickest route back to the car.

"Yeah."

"So, let's drop in and say hi then." She checked her watch and nudged him with her shoulder. He wasn't always her partner on cases. It just depended on who was free and how big a case it was, but they always worked well together, and she always nabbed him if he was free. As far as she was concerned, they got results and *that* was all that mattered. Over time she had learnt a lot about his private life and vice versa.

Dale Saint was head over heels in love with his partner. They weren't married – not that he hadn't asked her enough times already, but Becky didn't seem to be in any rush to tie herself down any more than two kids and busy career already did.

"I guess we could get lunch in the cafeteria." He grinned back and pulled out his phone, rattling off a quick text to let Becky know they were there. "Thanks, Guv."

~Doll~

The smell of the cafeteria always reminded her of school dinners; there was something nostalgic about it, and yet it was nauseating too. They had to queue up behind doctors, nurses, and patients with their trays that were shoved along the metal shelf until they finally reached the point at which someone was serving food. To be fair, this was one of the better places to eat, and they each loaded up with a jacket potato and salad. Just as they had sat down at a table still covered in someone else's leftovers, a short, thin woman, waved them over. She had long blonde hair, tied back neatly, and was wearing a pair of light blue scrubs. Becky was a theatre nurse on the surgical team, and she wasn't alone. Next to her stood another woman in identical scrubs, both hands firmly in the front pocket of her tunic. She was taller than Becky by several inches. Her hair was blonde too, but with a darker hue, flashes of red and gold streaked naturally through it. If asked for a description then Sophie would have to say she was attractive - *very* attractive. She wasn't skinny; curvaceous was the word – curves in all the right places. She smiled down at the detectives, dimples in either cheek. It was then that Sophie noted the blonde's cheeks blushed a little under her scrutiny.

"Hello Detectives." Becky giggled and bent to kiss Dale on the cheek. "Working hard are we?" Her eyebrow raised slightly as she checked out the plates of food they had been devouring. She had been on at Dale to eat something healthier for ages; he was starting to develop a paunch.

"You know us Becks, always on the go." Sophie replied. "You joining us or just standing around looking pretty?" She kept a straight face as she looked between Becky and her friend, her gaze lingering just long enough that the as-yet-unnamed woman noticed.

"I guess we could join you, seeing as we came all this way." Becky pulled a chair over from the table behind. "This is Rachel...she's kinda new, so be nice," she warned.

"We're always nice," Dale argued with a grin, his fork halfway between his plate and mouth.

"Not you, your surly partner over there." Becky winked at Whitton as the dark-haired detective took a bite of her lunch and looked up. "Her bark is worse than her bite," Becky added, turning to Rachel.

"Oh, I am sure the detective isn't anywhere near as bad as you make out," Rachel replied, her eyes firmly fixed on Sophie as she spoke. Her words sent a delicious shiver down Sophie's spine and the cop held her gaze again, until Dale coughed gently.

"Do you want me to get you anything?" he asked them both, half standing. Rachel turned her attention slowly toward him. "Like a room?" he mumbled out of the side of his mouth so only Sophie could hear him. She said nothing and continued eating.

"Oh, no thank you. Brought it with me." Rachel smiled and swung her bag around from over her shoulder to the table, producing a plastic lunch box and a flask. "Never know when you'll get the chance to eat so, always be prepared." Her attention was back on Whitton, who was continuing to eat like she was ravenous and hadn't been fed for a week.

"That's what I keep telling him," Whitton mumbled around her mouthful. "Bone saws don't agree with him though." She laughed as Dale flung his fork down on the plate.

"Really, Guv?" He glared, and she couldn't help but smirk as Rachel looked back and forth between them quizzically, waiting for Becky to fill her in.

"Payback's a bitch," she mumbled so only he could hear.

Oblivious to the detectives playing tit for tat, Becky explained to Rachel, "If they're here, it's either because one of them got hurt, the person they were after got hurt, or...they were at an autopsy." She looked at Dale, whose once healthy-looking features were now a sallow shade of yellow. "And judging by my beloved's face, it's the latter." She shrugged and produced her own box of culinary delights.

"What case are you working on?" Rachel asked. Whitton just looked at her.

"We uh, can't really say too much," Dale offered, and Rachel smiled at him. "Ya know how it is?"

She nodded knowingly before turning back to Sophie. "I heard on the radio that the Doll Maker's latest victim was found last night," she continued as she unwrapped a sandwich from its Clingfilm constraints.

"The what?" Sophie snorted.

"The Doll Maker, that's what they're calling him now." Once again, she held the detective's gaze and smiled slowly. "Must be pretty grim. I don't envy you." Sophie nodded, her resolve to remain truculent wavering slightly. "Maybe you can tell me about it sometime, over coffee."

Chapter Seven

Emma Taylor's body had been found on a Monday night, at 8:30 p.m. or there about. There was a parking space outside of the pub, and the following Monday night, Detective Inspector Whitton parked her car in it. She had a perfect view of the alley, and a hunch.

It was quiet on the main road. Stanford Street was usually only bustling when it was a weekend and the youth of the area ventured out to all the bars and clubs on offer. Mondays in a pub like the Bull would likely be a few locals and maybe some diehard quiz fanatics, but that would be about it until the Christmas rush brought with it party revellers and celebrations.

There was no real reason why Sophie Whitton was sitting out here on her own in the car at 8 p.m., just that nagging feeling that there was something here they were missing. She lit a cigarette and inhaled deeply while she cracked the window open a little so the smoke could dissipate. It was getting colder outside; winter was moving in fast.

Headlights appeared in her rear view mirror. A car was slowing and indicating. It pulled in behind her. She watched as two people clambered out, laughing and giggling as the passenger, a woman, tottered around the front of the car and grabbed the driver's hand. They then virtually ran hand in hand together into the pub. "Fuck sake," she mumbled and took another drag on her cigarette. She checked the clock on the dashboard: 8:12 p.m. The phone beeped, signalling a new text message had come through.

Yvonne: Hey, what time will you be home?

She started to reply and was halfway through explaining it would be a late one when another set of lights appeared. This time they were in front of her, pulling into the kerb before slowly reversing and turning into the alley.

Text message forgotten, she climbed out of the car and ran around the corner into the alleyway. The car had parked at the very end. The lights were switched off, and it was almost pitch black other than the small illumination from the interior light before it too was switched off. Two people were going at it, mouths devouring one another as they fought to remove each other's clothing. Whitton stuck closely to the wall, lurking in the shadow as she inched further into the alley, her keen eye taking in as much information as she could. The man looked to be in his 50s. He had short greying hair, slicked back to reveal a receding hairline. Bulky in his build, but not overweight. His companion on the other hand was much younger, early twenties. Her tight ponytail gave a sharp, pinched look to an overly made up face. She had tiny tits and a scrawny frame. The girl from behind the bar was fucking the landlord.

Whitton stepped out from the shadows and knocked on the driver's side window just as the girl was bending over his crotch. A blow job in a back alley; romance was clearly alive and kicking. She rolled her eyes and reminded herself to take a long shower when she finally got home.

He turned at once to the sharp tapping, wide-eyed and ready to tell whoever it was to piss off until he realised at once that it was the police. Pushing the girl away, he quickly yanked up his trousers and made himself presentable.

"Get out," Whitton ordered as she opened the door. The stench of weed wafting out mixed with perfume and overpowering aftershave; nauseating. She waited in silence for him to climb out of the car. The young girl went to follow. "Not you, you stay right there."

"Officer..." His face tried to smile, but the nerves shone right through it.

"Detective," she reminded him. "Detective Inspector Whitton, you might remember me? I'm the one dealing with the murder of Emma Taylor."

"Of course, of course...I...this isn't, I mean..." He scrabbled about for an explanation. Caught with his pants down in a sordid little romance down a back alley. He couldn't be more embarrassed.

"I don't care who you're fucking, Mr. Harding. Unless you was fucking Emma Taylor too?" She looked him square in the eye and studied him. He was a squealer, she was sure of it. Nothing would remain a secret. She would know what time he took a dump if she asked him.

"No, absolutely not, no...Erica and I..." He turned back to the car, a small grin appearing as he glanced at the girl. "Erica and I, we're...well, we're in love."

Sophie raised a brow and nodded. "Right."

"And well...as you know, Mrs Harding doesn't..." He swallowed at the thought of his wife. "She wouldn't like it, obviously..." The sex life of the middle-aged bar manager really was the last thing Sophie wanted an image of.

"How long?"

"Sorry?"

"How long have you been shagging?" she asked more succinctly.

"I don't see how that's..." His face flushed a deep purple. He was going to try and hide something. Idiot. She slammed her palm into the side of his face and pushed his head against the roof of the car.

"Was you fucking Erica the night Emma was murdered?" He fidgeted and tried to free himself, but she pushed harder. "Mr Harding." She spoke more firmly, got his attention and stepped right up into his face. "I ain't interested in anything other than catching Emma's killer, but if you or Erica are hiding something then I will drag both of you down the station and throw every indecency charge I can find at the pair of you, do I make myself clear?"

"Y-yes. Look, we didn't...it's not like we can identify him or anything." Her blood was rushing as she listened to him. Her heart thumped as the information infiltrated her brain and settled neatly into place.

"You *saw* him?"

"I don't know...it was dark and we were...busy." He blushed. She reached behind and unhooked the handcuffs that she kept dangling on her belt. "Okay, okay...look all I know is that on that night, we were parked like we are now and well...this other car reversed in and parked. Next thing I know, someone came running out of the yard and jumped back into the car and drove off." Whitton thought about it, pictured the scene and imagined the car parked just 30 or so feet in front.

"Why didn't you see him get out of the car? What caused him to come running out like that?" She was talking to herself, but a voice from inside the car spoke up.

"For fuck sake it's freezing, just tell her!" When Harding stayed silent, Erica piped up again. "He was too busy getting a blow job." Erica smirked, seemingly proud of herself. "I hit the horn by accident, ya know when he got to the point of..."

"Yeah, yeah I don't need a description," Sophie snarled, cutting her off.

"Anyway, two minutes later a figure came running out and jumped in the car," Harding continued. "We didn't see his face.

"But you saw the car!" she barked. He flinched and nodded. "Well? Colour, make?"

"It was white. A saloon, a Ford maybe." She jotted it down in her notebook.

"I want the pair of you at the station first thing. I don't care what you tell your missus, but I need statements. Emma *needs* your statements." She turned then and left them both to consider just how much shit they were in.

Chapter Eight

Opening the door, she couldn't help but notice the wonderful aroma of something delicious being cooked. Kicking off her shoes and shrugging off her jacket, Sophie made her way into the kitchen and found Yvonne sitting at the dining table. A wine glass in her hand swilled blood red as she moved it rhythmically in circles. The half-empty bottle to her left stood accusingly next to an empty plate, which in turn sat opposite another empty plate. Her lover didn't speak. Instead, she took another sip of her drink and placed the glass down gently on the placemat. Her fingers lightly caressed the stem as though it were her lover, rather than the figure standing in front of her.

"I thought that maybe tonight, of all nights, that you might have made it home a little earlier." She sat back in her chair, her voice calm; too calm. Her auburn hair was neat and tidy as usual. She had made an extra effort with it, though. Even her make-up had been touched up, and she was wearing a floral dress, something Sophie was sure was new. "I hoped that maybe, just maybe, tonight would be more important than your *sodding* job!" There were tears now. She rose from her seat, her voice rising along with her. "Do I have to get myself fucking murdered to get your attention!? Is that it!?"

Sophie had realised far too late exactly what she had done. She had spent her evening witnessing a sordid little love affair down a back alley instead of being here, at home, celebrating their anniversary. She kicked herself internally. How could she forget?

She had even set a reminder on her calendar. "I'm sorry, I just got caught up..."

"You're always 'just caught up.'" Yvonne made air quotes with her fingers in the most sarcastic manner she could manage. Sighing heavily, she took her seat again, along with a swig of her wine, emptying the glass. "Four years Sophie, four years of building this life together, and for what? You don't come home, and when you do you're not here, not really. There's always a case, always something you just need to check."

"I know, I'm sorry...I really am, but it's important."

"Don't!" She held up a hand, palm flat out, towards Sophie's face. "Don't tell me it's important when I so clearly am not." The chair she had been sitting in fell backwards, crashing to the floor behind her, when she stood, angry and pissed off.

"I'm not saying that...You *know* you're important."

"Do I?" She stood there for a moment just glaring at her: DI Whitton, the woman she fell in love with and whom she wanted to spend her life with, raise a family with. "Something needs to change, Sophie."

"Why is this all about me? You're not exactly..."

"I'm not exactly what?" Yvonne twisted back around to face her. "Go on, say what you're thinking, Sophie!" They stood staring at one another, anger and frustration bubbling away beneath the surface.

"I'm not doing this right now, Yvonne," Sophie said. Pouring a glass of wine, she swallowed it down in one go.

"Fine." She wasn't fine; she was anything but fine. *They* were anything but fine.

~Doll~

There were over 70,000 Ford Focuses sold the previous year alone in the UK. To say it was a needle in a haystack was an understatement. But the car they were looking for wasn't a new one, and it had a black bumper and tinted windows, which narrowed it down considerably. That was according to Don Harding and his statement. How reliable that was when he was mid-orgasm in the front seat of his car, Saint wasn't clear on, but it was something, and it was more than they had had previously.

"You look like shit boss, heavy night?" Dale said, dropping down into the seat next to Whitton.

"Something like that," she muttered, taking a drag on a cigarette that was almost finished. She pulled out the pack and lit a new one off the old and then flicked it out into the street. She passed the pack to Dale, who took one and lit it. "So, he wears a hat, drives a shitty old car and looks to be about 6 foot, that about it?"

"Pretty much." He inhaled. "At least now though we can search CCTV and see if we can pick him up anywhere...ya never know?"

"Yeah, ya never know," she agreed, exhaling. "You ever think about packing it all in, the job I mean?" she asked him, staring straight ahead as she took another drag.

"Doesn't everyone?" he returned with a smirk. "Let's face it, it's the shit part of society we deal with most of the time. Who wouldn't consider jacking it all in?"

"Yeah, I guess so." She stood up, brushing the ash off of her coat, and dropped the cigarette to the floor so her size 7 boots could crush it. "All of Barnard's little minions have reported back, we should drop by and see if there is anything interesting."

~Doll~

The car park at Woodington University Hospital was packed as usual. All official spaces, and some that were not supposed to be parking spaces, were filled with vehicles of visitors and staff. They drove around it twice in the hope that somebody would pull out, but they were out of luck. There was sometimes a space for police cars and personnel over by the mortuary, but it was already taken by another squad car..

"Sod it, just park at main entrance. I'm not fucking around all afternoon looking for a space," Whitton huffed, rolling her shoulders. That couch really wasn't comfortable for sleeping on. She was tired, and that made her irritable.

They walked through the revolving doors that led through to reception. Taking a left, they followed the red, blue, and yellow lines on the floor that would lead them to the other side of the building. Once there they turned right and took the stairs down one floor, one step at a time until they followed a green line that took them to the back exit.

"DI Whitton, nice to see you again...Detective Saint." Rachel nodded briefly at Dale before turning her attention back to Sophie. "So, what brings you back to Woodington?" She smiled, her lips covered in a thin sheen of pink gloss, all shiny and kissable.

"Oh, you know, the usual."

"Sounds...ominous. Do you ever smile, Detective?" Sophie looked away and caught Dale grinning out the corner of her eye.

"Sometimes, generally not when I'm trying to catch a serial killer." She held the woman's gaze, attempting to appear disinterested. She wasn't so sure she had succeeded.

Unperturbed, Rachel continued. "You strong silent types are always worth the wait." She winked and moved past them both before turning. "That offer of coffee still stands."

Dale Saint bit his bottom lip and scrunched up his nose. "So, want me to get Becky to tell her to back off?"

"Nah, I'm a big girl. I can handle a nurse's crush." She rubbed the back of her neck. "Anyway." She sniffed. The cold weather outside mixed with the warmth of the building making her nose run. "I ain't got time for Yvonne, let alone a hot nurse on the prowl." They pushed through the doors and held them open for a porter to wheel in a trolley.

"Thanks," He mumbled as he trundled off, looking back at them over his shoulder.

"Don't tell Becky I said this, but..." He looked around just to make sure Becky wasn't within earshot. "Rachel is fucking sexy, ya got to admit it."

"Yeah, she is." Sophie confirmed, subconsciously looking back in the direction the woman had walked and only making eye contact with the scruffy porter.

Chapter Nine

Dr Barnard's office was the complete opposite of anywhere else in the building. The furniture was antique and the décor just as antiquated, the design clearly in keeping with his favourite era. The room was dominated by an Edwardian rosewood inlaid suite. Two armchairs and a two-seater settee placed in the centre of the room surrounded a French Marquetry coffee table. On top of it was an engraved silver salver that held a matching silver teapot and three bone china cups with saucers. Sophie knew all this because over time, Tristan had informed her of all the details. She enjoyed his quirks.

"I don't know about you, but I am parched. Tea?" he asked, lowering his bulk into the chair. He looked a little out of place in the room and yet, so very at home.

"Thanks." Dale smiled from across the table. Sophie shook her head with a polite no. She rarely drank tea – coffee, lager, or something stronger were her go-tos.

"Did you find anything?" she asked instead, all business.

"Straight to the point as usual, DI Whitton." He smiled. "Okay, well there really wasn't much that the cadaver could tell us other than what I've already conveyed, but..." He smiled again as the detectives sat forward, Dale balancing his cup and saucer on his knee. "We did find a hair, and it matches the tearstain. Now, there isn't a DNA match currently in the system, but you bring me something to test and we will know one way or the other if the person is related."

"Yes!" Dale shouted, his cup and saucer rattling, drawing a nervous glance from the doctor.

"Careful Detective, that is a vintage fine bone china tea cup balanced precariously upon your bony knee." Dale took hold of it with two hands and placed it safely back on the table. "Now, what else I can tell you is that the man you are looking for is a European Caucasian and a redhead, and he either smokes or is around a cannabis smoker on a regular basis."

"You got all that from one hair?" Dale asked as Sophie added all the information to her notebook. Tristan raised a brow and nodded.

"What else, Doc?" Sophie asked, his gaze turning back to her in an instant, a wry smile on his face.

"You know me too well, Detective. I have your dead girl's name."

~Doll~

Whitton placed a new photograph on the murder board. It sat to the right of two others. Anjelika Tyzska, Emma Taylor, and now, Sandra Bancroft.

"Sandra Bancroft, 34 years old. Single mother to Noah. She's originally from Sheffield, but had moved south for work and because Noah's father's family lived nearby. Her own family history is somewhat sketchy. In and out of care for most of her life," Sophie explained to the room. "From what little we know, she often took Noah to Copers Field to meet Alex Jenson, the father. He would take Noah for a few days while Sandra was working. Then they would meet up again and Noah would spend time with his mum again." She pointed to a picture of a smiling Alex Jenson that was pinned beneath Sandra. "On Friday night Mr. Jenson met Sandra at approximately 6:45 p.m. They talked for roughly fifteen minutes about Noah and made tentative arrangements to go on a date; they were apparently talking about getting back together."

"Is he a suspect, guv?" Andy Bowen called out from the back of the room.

"As far as I and anyone in this room is concerned, until we catch this bastard, *everyone* is a suspect!" She shrugged her jacket off and placed it around the back of the nearest chair. "Mr. Jenson said that he watched her walk towards the path until she was out of sight and then he took Noah home, which is where he remains at present."

"Poor little lad," someone else mumbled.

"So, the body was found on Sunday evening. According to the Doc she was dead at least 48 hours. Our assumption is that she met the killer at approximately 7 p.m. Friday night and that sometime after that she was murdered, tortured, and then placed where she was found. What I want right now is for every member of this team to get to work and start digging through CCTV. Find the nearest cameras, check them all, and log every single person that goes anywhere near that cut through. I want CCTV checked for the car. Ask the wardens if they issued any tickets. I want another house-to-house; ask about the car and the description we have."

~Doll~

Jeff Branson was an experienced cop in his early forties. He knew the job inside and out, and if given a task, he followed it through, which was why Whitton put him on the CCTV search for the car.

He had been at it for two days solid, slowly following the car from the first point that it was picked up on Stanford St. Unfortunately, none of the CCTV had been good enough to focus in on the registration plate. It was either a terrible quality recording, or the weather had made it grainy with the constant rain and sleet recently. He had followed the vehicle from the scene of Emma Taylor's murder, taking a left and then a right before he lost it. It was a slow and painstaking process having to go through every tape of CCTV from every shop, bar, or private video source. The police had even made a plea for anyone with a dash cam who was in the area that night, and on the other nights when the other two victims were slaughtered, to come forward.

"Guv," Jeff called out across the busy room from his desk, a pen gripped between his teeth. The entire space in front of him was filled with tapes and DVDs from every possible business in a five-mile area. To his left sat the pile he had already searched through; the other, much larger pile he still had to look at loomed to his right. "I've picked him up again. He is heading out toward Tate's Green." The constant buzz of conversation went silent as everybody looked up from whatever they were doing and gave Branson their attention.

"Great, keep on it Jeff. Somewhere this bastard is going to fuck up, and when he does..." She left it unsaid, but they all knew the sentiment. She checked her watch; just gone seven p.m. If she left now, she could be home in twenty minutes and spend the evening with Yvonne. Glancing around the room, she could see the team hard at it. Each one of them was following up a lead or chasing down an answer, giving up an evening at home with their own loved ones. It was expected; that was just what you did when you joined C.I.D. They all knew that, accepted it. So did she usually, but she wouldn't feel guilty tonight.

She grabbed her keys from the desk drawer and slammed it shut. "I'll be on the end of the phone if anyone needs me," she called out as she made a decision and left for the evening.

Chapter Ten

Breathless and wet with perspiration and arousal, she writhed as she felt the delightful touch of her lover's fingers and mouth, hot against her skin as they grazed and charted her body in the way only a knowing lover can. Her back arched as her lover found glory with her tongue, expertly circling her, sucking and lapping until her breath was stilled and her body tensed. Her hips pulsing as she fought to hold off the inevitable climax for just a few seconds more.

Sophie arriving home before eight had been a surprise. Sophie taking Yvonne to bed and making love to her was an even bigger astonishment, one she wasn't going to complain about. They had fallen into a comfortable state that had threatened to become stale, and if she was honest, their relationship was running out of steam. After the argument the other night, she wasn't sure any longer if Sophie even wanted to be here, but now, as she felt her lover explore her depths and taste her in ways she hadn't done in months, she felt a reassurance that maybe there was hope for them to fix things.

"Not that I am complaining..." Yvonne began as she nestled into Sophie's arms. "But, what brought that on?"

"I figured it was long overdue." Sophie pressed her lips against her lover's head and breathed her in. Remnants of coconut and lime mixed with Chanel – a welcoming aroma.

"Mm, it was, and very welcome." Yvonne kissed the bare shoulder beneath her. "Thank you."

"We should probably do this more often," Sophie suggested.

"Yes, yes we should." She rolled forward and lifted herself to hover above the dark-haired detective. Straddling the firm thigh, she sank down and thrust slowly. "No reason why we shouldn't start now."

"I guess not."

The kiss was languid. Sophie always wanted to take control, and Yvonne was happy to let her. She was determined to be unhurried and enjoy this sudden and unexpected opportunity in its entirety.

~Doll~

Yvonne had been asleep for a little over an hour. Sophie had spent the time staring at the ceiling. Physically satisfied, she would normally fall asleep easily, but her monkey chatter just wouldn't switch off. She was hot and kicked the covers off, the cool air of the night easily wrapping itself around her naked form. After a while a shiver crawled across her and she let it slowly chill her bones, imagining the last minutes of Sandra Bancroft's life as it seeped away from her into a frozen abyss. Her last thoughts were probably of a small boy with sandy white curls. Then she thought about the other two. All of them were blonde, all petite like young girls – like teenagers, but older. He definitely had a type, she just wasn't sure exactly why.

Her phone vibrated on the bedside table to her right and she grabbed it quickly, not wanting to disturb Yvonne. She got up to answer it.

"Where you going?" Yvonne mumbled, her face squashed against her pillow.

"Go back to sleep...it's just work." She had hesitated to tell her, knowing it would piss her off. She needn't have worried. Von was asleep again within seconds as she crept out of the room, swiping the screen to answer as she moved. "Whitton."

~Doll~

They had found the car. According to Detective Constable Branson, it was the car. He had followed it from Stanford Street through Tate's Green and picked it up again out on the dual carriageway where it had turned off. He lost it for a while, but then picked it up again as it headed back towards Woodington. It then parked on a side street, and it was still there.

"Okay, so what have we got?" Whitton asked Branson and Saint as she strode into the office, unwinding her scarf as she moved.

"We've sent a car down to drive past and double check it's the car we're looking for. We're just waiting now for confirmation," Branson replied. The grin on his face was bright enough to light up the darkened room. He was a good-looking guy. With ebony skin and dark, smiling eyes, he looked like the kind of guy who waited tables in Hollywood while waiting for his big break.

"Alright, good work guys." There was something tangible in the air around them: hope. "Coffees are on me." She pulled a tenner out of her pocket and thrust it into Dale's hand. "It's your turn to go." She laughed at his pout. The tension in the air had lifted.

It didn't last though. The call came in thirty minutes later with the news that it wasn't the car they were looking for.

"Fuck it!" she shouted and threw her phone across the room. "When are we going to get a fucking break?"

Dale bent down and picked up the tossed mobile. He rubbed the screen across his trouser leg and wiped off all the dust, inspecting it for any cracks. "It's not broken," he said, passing it back to her.

"Thanks," she mumbled, tossing it down on the desk. "It's been two weeks, nearly three already since Sandra. It took 5 months between one and two, but only three between two and three. He is escalating."

"What about Doc's theory on the three wise monkeys?" Dale asked. "Three, that could be it...he could be done."

He had a point, but Whitton wasn't so sure that it was that simple.

Chapter Eleven

He watched her asking her questions and stomping around like she owned the place. She didn't; this was his world and she knew nothing about it, had no understanding of what motivated him. Why would she? She hadn't lived it.

He'd read the papers; watched the news often. He saw what they were calling him The Doll Maker; he quite liked it. Tiffany would like it. She had loved her doll. They didn't have a clue. None of them did.

They had no idea how long he had planned for this, how time-consuming it was to make each doll exactly how he needed it to be. He didn't choose anyone, no; they always seemed to find him. Like it was meant to be. They were unique in that they were just like...her, how she would look now. His face crumpled remembering the day his mother told him she was gone. She had taken her own life. He had wanted to see her, but they wouldn't let him, said he was too young. He didn't remember a funeral either; he was sent back to school the minute she could palm him off. He begged to stay, but they wouldn't hear of it.

They hadn't even found the first one yet, the one that had set him on this path. Maybe once they did they would work it out, but he doubted it. He hadn't known he needed to do this until the first. That one was out of anger really, but once he had done it and thought about it, it all made sense. He finally understood the reason why she had come into his life. Fucking her had been fun at first; so what if he had had to pay for it at times, or if she was ancient. It was a means to an end, until he had realised why she was attractive to him, and then he had vomited. Puked his dinner all over the bed. Strangely, he hadn't been ill when he had killed her.

The first one they *had* found had been so perfect, angelic-looking and beautiful – exactly how he envisioned she would be. His memories of her were so vivid still. Long blonde hair and a slim physique, midway through her teens, she was still yet to blossom – and she never would.

It was so simple. He knew at once that she was the one. All he had had to do was knock on her door, and she had just let him in. As easy as that. As though she had known him her entire life.

The second one though, that had pissed him off. The whole thing had been in the planning for weeks, and it was a monumental fuck up. It had pissed him off that he hadn't had as much time with her to treat her properly. But, she was perfect. Just like his beloved Tiffany.

He had watched her for days. Every shift she had, he was there: watching. He knew her pattern. Arrive at work early to go and get changed, then have a ciggie out the back before getting behind the bar and smiling at him. He had had a lot of plans for her, plans he had to forget about when that blasted car horn went off. It was too big of a risk to get caught before he had finished his work.

Number three had been his favourite. She had looked so peaceful when he was finished with her. She was the most like Tiffany of them all so far. He had waited days for her to go somewhere alone. That kid was always with her. He watched her with the kid and almost changed his mind about her. But then she sent the kid away and he took his opportunity.

Now, he was watching again. It wouldn't be long.

Then they would all see and understand.

Chapter Twelve

The days and then weeks passed slowly. The Chief Inspector, along with Whitton and Dr. Barnard, took part in a televised appeal for information. Sophie hated these; she didn't see the point on the whole. They would be inundated with hundreds of calls, all requiring manpower that could be used elsewhere. She could guarantee at least three psychics would call in offering up names that the dead girls, now in spirit, had given them, and of course the usual nutters claiming responsibility. No real leads came from it.

With nothing more to go on, they had little choice but to wait it out and hope that at best, he had stopped, and whatever it was that was driving him had somehow been concluded, but they knew that that wasn't likely. People like him didn't start killing and then just stop, unless they were dead or imprisoned for something else maybe.

On the home front, things were no easier. Frustration incorporated with exhaustion had meant that even when Sophie was at home, it was difficult. Long gone was the night of passion that Yvonne had hung her hopes on.

"Jeremy and Paul are coming over tonight for dinner," she reminded Sophie. "You won't be late, will you?"

"Of course...I'll do my best," Sophie replied, ripping the corner of a piece of toast with her teeth and chewing noisily. Yvonne took a shaky breath and turned to face her.

"If you don't...then don't bother coming home." She spoke firmly and held the gaze that glared at her. "I mean it Sophie, this has been planned for weeks. We've been talking about this for months."

~Doll~

Suffocating, that's how it felt to be at her desk today. If she read those files once more she would literally explode with frustration. It felt like karma was deliberately thwarting her at every turn. Yvonne was pissed off again, which to be fair she kind of understood. She was never home, and Yvonne was at the end of her tether, but that just made it a catch 22 because the more annoyed Yvonne became, the less Sophie wanted to go home. Dale was pissy and annoying too. Most of the team had moved on to other cases for the moment. And now, it was snowing outside.

The window sill had caught several inches of it as it crept up the glass pane, blocking the view of the building next door. Whitton had her feet up on the corner of her desk and was spending her time ripping up a piece of waste paper and screwing it up into tiny balls that she could flick across the room towards the bin. Another hour and she would be at home discussing sperm donations. A phone rang out, but she didn't care; it wasn't hers. She half listened as Dale answered and replied accordingly with whatever it was the person on the other end was saying. She almost got whiplash when Dale was shouting at her. "We've got another one...and *he's* alive."

"*He*?! Fuck!" She was up and on her feet instantly, pulling on her coat as she met him by the door. "Alive?"

"Yeah. He's being taken to the hospital."

"Let's go."

~Doll~

They dumped the car in a space marked "Ambulance," left the blue lights flashing as a sign of emergency, and literally ran into Accident & Emergency. The A&E department was heaving. It was a Friday afternoon, but that didn't seem to have made a difference on the amount of people waiting to be seen by emergency doctors.

"DI Whitton and DS Saint, we need to speak to the man brought in..." She flashed her warrant card and nudged Dale to do the same.

"The Doll Maker vic?" The receptionist seemed almost gleeful to be caught up in something that was obviously exciting to her. Whitton glowered at her.

"The attempted *murder* victim," she stated through gritted teeth. "Where is he?"

"There's no need to take that tone with me, Officer." She was a thin woman. So thin that Whitton considered several ways in which she could break her scrawny neck if she didn't give up the information in the next 20 seconds. She was saved from any potential murder of her own, however, when a voice piped up from behind.

"Detective, I see you've lost none of your charm." Whitton spun around and found Rachel within a foot of her, smirking. "Would you like me to show you where you need to go?" Whitton nodded and began to follow, Saint tagging along behind, but not before she had thrown a last glare back at the irritating woman on reception.

"I'm not sure he is going to be much help to you at the moment. He's in surgery, there's a swelling on his brain. He also...glued his hands to a vodka bottle. He's been beaten pretty badly too, and he wasn't conscious when he arrived either." Whitton appreciated the professional approach Rachel was taking. She didn't mind the flirting, but there was a time and a place for it; this wasn't it.

~Doll~

An hour and a half later, Dale Saint was on his way to the actual crime scene. Someone needed to confirm that the doll they found at the scene was the same as the others. It wasn't like there was anything he could do here; the unknown man was still in surgery and likely would be for a while longer. Whitton would rather have Dale out there with his ear to the ground, sniffing out what went down and how, than sitting around here drinking coffee and moaning that he could be doing something more useful. They needed confirmation that it was definitely the Doll Maker and not some sick copycat.

The plastic chair she sat in was the most uncomfortable contraption ever invented. Five identical green bucket seats were screwed to a metal bar frame that was then screwed to the floor. Frustrated beyond belief, and with her arse numb, she stood and began pacing the corridor. She needed a cigarette. Patting down her pockets, she found the pack, pulled one out, and headed for the exit.

Outside it was bitterly cold. The weather had definitely turned wintry overnight. Standing in a doorway to try and shield herself as well as the lighter, she took a long drag and blew the smoke out and up into the air. Her inquisitive mind was jumping from one question to the next, and none of them had any answers yet.

"You know that's not good for you, right?" Rachel appeared from nowhere and stood right in front of her, observing. Sophie looked at her and then the cigarette before laying her eyes back on the concerned face of the blonde nurse.

"Yeah. It's gonna kill me one day." She nodded, her voice dry and lacking anything but sarcasm. She rubbed the back of her neck. Her spine was stiff, and the idea of dying was almost pleasant.

"Well, yes probably, but that wasn't what I was talking about." She stepped closer, pulling her jacket more tightly around herself. "I was talking about the stress, it's written all over you."

Sophie almost laughed out loud, but instead she snorted derisorily. "That's the life of a cop for ya." She took another drag.

Rachel held her hand out and confidently took the cigarette from Whitton's fingers. She took a pull on it, blowing the smoke out and into Sophie's face.

"Same for nurses," she said as she passed the half-smoked cigarette back to the copper and smiled. "He isn't going to be out of surgery for a while yet, and even then, he's going to be heavily sedated."

Sophie nodded. "I know."

"So why are you still here?" Rachel asked. She moved closer to the intense woman, appraising her as she took her in. Detective Inspector Whitton was a tad taller than herself. Her short, dark mop of hair was hidden for now under the hood of her jacket, which also covered the fact she was skin and bone, unlike Rachel's womanlier hourglass figure. There was an intensity about her that the nurse liked and found herself drawn to and aroused by. Underneath all that brooding seriousness was a passion who just needed an outlet; she was sure of it.

Their eyes met and held. There was a connection there; both could feel it, though Sophie would deny it if asked. "Because until we ID him he has nobody, and everybody deserves to have somebody." She looked away and took one last drag before she flicked the butt to the ground and stomped on it.

~Doll~

Saint called with an update. The dolls matched. The victim was Gary Price. Forty-eight years old, he had celebrated his birthday just ten days earlier. A mature student at the local college studying sociology and mathematics. He had a boyfriend that he had been planning to meet later that evening; he never made it.

After ringing around everyone he knew and finding that nobody had seen Gary since his last class, Brian Hogan got anxious and called the police. The Doll Maker headlines had everybody on edge and with the description of petite, blonde woman, the boyfriend had never assumed his lover could be in any danger, he had just assumed an accident. Gary's route from uni into town took him over the bridge of the river wooding. He had stopped off at a pub – according to the receipt found in his pocket – and had a couple of drinks before heading down a towpath that ran parallel to the river, and that was where he was found: folded up in the fetal position like a small child with his hands out in front of him as if he were praying, and glued between the palms was a bottle of Vodka that had been poured down his throat. His shirt was drenched in the stuff.

"His parents have arrived. So has the boyfriend," Rachel said, breaking her from her thoughts. She had her coat on once more and had swapped her uniform for jeans and a sweater. A woolen hat was in her hand, ready to pull down over her head. "Wanna get that coffee?"

Sophie glanced at her watch; 9:15 p.m. She had been here for over four hours, missed dinner and was well and truly in the doghouse. She couldn't face going home right now and dealing with the fall-out from Yvonne. Her palm slid slowly over her face as she contemplated the monumental fuck up her life had become.

Before she could answer, a tall man in another uniform paused as he passed. He looked first at Sophie and then at Rachel. Whitton recognised him as the porter that had held the door open for herself and Saint on an earlier visit.

"Hi Rachel, had a good day?" he said, stammering his way through the simple sentence.

"Yeah, exhausting as usual, but it's looking up now." She smiled, but her eyes moved from him to the detective and lingered there.

"Yeah, course. I was wondering if..." He fidgeted from one foot to the other and Sophie ignored the urge to just push him out of the way.

"I'm sorry, Pete, isn't it? I really need to get going. The detective here is buying me coffee."

"Oh, right, yeah course, no problem...another time maybe." He looked away; poor sod had probably taken weeks to pluck up the courage.

"Sure...I like ya hair by the way. You've bleached it, right?"

He grinned like a kid at the compliment and the fact that she had noticed. He raised his hand to brush through his scruffy overgrown locks. Whatever bleach he had used hadn't done a great job. It was still orange in places where the colour hadn't quite been stripped.

"Thanks." He blushed a little before turning and briskly walking away.

"Admirer?" Sophie asked.

"Well, as strange as it might seem to you, Detective Surly, I am a catch." She turned herself now and looking over her shoulder she said, "Come on."

Chapter Thirteen

The drive over had been quiet. Whitton followed the directions that Rachel gave and found herself pulling into the driveway of a small cottage in a tiny village on the outskirts of town.

"I thought we were going for coffee?"

"We are." Rachel winked and opened the passenger side door. "I didn't say where we were going." She climbed out before Sophie could question her any further and walked up to the arched front door, her key sliding into the lock effortlessly.

Whitton sat still for a moment. What was she doing here? Playing with fire, that's what she was doing. She climbed out, closed the car door quietly, and followed the other woman inside.

The cottage was cosy, warm and inviting. Nothing matched; it was an eclectic jumble of furniture and knickknacks collected over time. Rachel watched the brooding woman as she stood just inside the doorway.

"You can come in," she laughed and wandered back into the kitchen, lifting the kettle to fill from the tap. Sophie stepped forwards and shook off her jacket. She looked around for somewhere to hang it. Finding nowhere suitable, she folded it neatly over the back of an armchair. Rachel came back into the room and pulled a chair out from the table, indicating she should sit there. Then the nurse moved about the room as Sophie watched. She flicked a switch and picked up an old vinyl record.

Placing it gently on the deck, she inched the arm across and dropped it softly. Soothing notes began to play out, and the dulcet tones of an 80's ballad floated around the room from its various speakers.

"I took a guess that you're a sugar and milk kind of woman," Rachel said, bringing two mugs to the table. She placed one in front of Sophie; Wonder Woman looked back at her from it. "I thought it was apt."

Sophie smirked, but remained quiet. They drank their coffee in relative silence. There was eye contact though, lots of it, and Sophie had the distinct feeling that she was being evaluated.

With her coffee finished, Rachel took her cup out to the kitchen. She rolled her head on her shoulders and watched Whitton from the doorway as she also stretched her neck from side to side. She closed her eyes and exhaled. It was the first time today that she had almost relaxed. She felt warm palms settle against her shoulder and stiffened instinctively, her eyes opening in an instant.

"You feel...tense, Detective." Sophie's eyes closed again as she felt the deft fingers begin to squeeze and pinch at the knots that had cultivated beneath her flesh over the past God-knows-how-many weeks, and she tightened her thighs at the intense shot of arousal that pulsed through her every time Rachel called her *'Detective.'*

Rachel's fingers trailed across her shoulders delicately as she circled the detective and came around to stand before her. Slowly she took a step closer, moving one leg either side of Sophie and lowering herself down onto her lap. The detective's hands automatically moved and took hold of Rachel's hips; to push her away or pull her closer, she wasn't sure just yet. "Why don't you let me help you relieve some of that?" Rachel's voice was barely a whisper; breathless and suggestive against her ear before her lips made contact with the soft skin just below Sophie's lobe.

Sophie hadn't even noticed the button to her trousers being undone or the zipper as it slid lower; she was so focused on this woman who seemed to see her for who she was. She hadn't even realised that she needed this until she felt Rachel's fingertips make contact and the involuntary thrust of her hips at the touch. She closed her eyes and let her head fall backwards as she exhaled.

Rachel smiled knowingly. "Let me help you," she whispered once more before bringing her lips to Whitton's throat.

She shouldn't be doing this. It was wrong on every level, and yet she felt powerless to stop it. She had Yvonne at home; they had a life together. She shouldn't want this, but she did. She should stop it now before it went too far, but she didn't. It already had.

There was nothing tentative about Rachel's movements, nothing inquiring or explorative. She knew what she was doing, had done this before; that much was clear.

Urgently, she reached around Rachel and drew her closer, burying her face between plump heaving breasts as she clung desperately to any sense of who she was.

"Just let go...Detective." Rachel smiled against her as their mouths finally met, knowing the effect her mouth was having on Sophie with her words and its movement. She grinned when she felt the forceful pull from Whitton as the detective's hips rose and fell, grinding against her, using her, forcing through the climax she so desperately needed right now.

~Doll~

Rachel's bed was as comfortable as any other Sophie had attempted to sleep in lately. The music had long since finished playing downstairs, and now all she could hear were the soft snuffling sounds of sleep from her bed partner.

She had just had the best sex of her life, and yet all she could think about was getting out of there. It was 3 o'clock in the morning, and she had work to do, and...a relationship to fix, but there was a part of her that just wanted to lie here and forget about everything else. Just hunker down under this duvet and pretend life was all okay, but she couldn't; too many things needed sorting.

Her clothes were still downstairs. As quietly as she could, she slipped out from under the warmth of the covers and crept naked down the cold, creaky stairs. Pulling her clothes on in the dark, she checked her phone: three missed messages.

The hospital: *Patient out of surgery and in recovery. Not to be disturbed for at least 12 hours.*

Dale Saint: *Can't see Gary for 12 hours! Fuck sake. Anyway, nothing much else to report other than the white car was seen in the area. I'm on it.*

Yvonne: *I really can't believe you would do this. You knew how important this was to me. Seriously Sophie, fuck you!*

If she had felt guilt two hours ago, then it was tenfold now as she crept out of the door and left without looking back.

Chapter Fourteen

Just before 4 a.m., Sophie crept around a different home: her own. She stepped into the shower and let the water wash over her, washing away the odor of sex, another woman's sex and touch. A touch that she had felt much deeper than she had initially expected, or wanted to admit.

She thought back to earlier, falling into bed with Rachel. Everything had been seamless as they had come together, arching in unison. When they had finally come to a halt, breathless and sated, they had talked; really talked. Rachel had been interested in her work, interested in her and how her day had been. She asked the right questions and stayed silent for the answers. It had been a long time since Yvonne had done that.

Dale was already in the office when he called her at 7 a.m. It was going to be a long and busy day working the case. She rubbed at her gritty eyes and blearily looked around the room. Yvonne was already gone. The apartment's silence was berating her; mocking her.

She still felt the guilt of it all weighing heavy on her shoulders and yet, she felt a lot lighter in herself than she had done previously.

~Doll~

Gary Price was out of it for nearly 30 hours. Jeff had managed to track the car for a while until once again, it just disappeared. Dale had found witnesses who had seen a tall man wearing a hoodie and a baseball cap running towards where the car was sighted. But that had led nowhere. As usual, they were running around chasing their tails and getting nowhere.

"He is awake, and you'll be able to speak with him for a little while, but bear in mind that painkillers and trauma will make this difficult for him," the doctor on duty had explained.

"Of course. We're not here to make things worse for him, but we do need to ask pertinent questions," Whitton explained. "He is the only person to have seen him and survived."

The doctor nodded. Everybody was aware of the importance Gary Price now had to this investigation.

They'd placed him in a private room. It wasn't the Hilton, but it was better than being on a ward full of nosy people that broke wind every five minutes and snored throughout the night. A standard hospital bed sat in the middle of the room. The TV monitor swung round from an arm attached to the wall behind, but he wasn't watching it. His parents sat opposite each other, one either side of the bed, looking shell-shocked. His mother placed her hand over one of his, the one that wasn't a pin cushion to drips and cannulas.

He had been lucky. The surgery team had been able to remove the bottle and the glue. His hands would be sore for a while as several layers of skin had been damaged in the process. His head injury was far more serious, but all in all, things could have been a lot worse for Gary Price.

"Hi Gary, my name is Detective Inspector Whitton, this is Detective Sargent Dale Saint. We're investigating what happened to you, would you be able to talk to us for a moment?" This was the worst part for Sophie: pushing a witness. Someone already dealing with the trauma of whatever crime had befallen them, and now they had to keep reliving it as police officers probed them for every tiny minute detail they might not even think was relevant.

"Sure." He nodded, eager to help right now, but it wouldn't be long before he felt exhausted by it all. He had a fat lip with a butterfly stitch, two black eyes and a cut across his nose, and his head was wrapped in a clean bandage like a turban. He had taken a beating.

"We'll just be outside, okay?" his mum said softly, leaning forward to kiss his cheek.

"Okay." He tried to smile, grimacing as his lip tugged at the stitch.

They all smiled solemnly as they passed each other, the parents moving towards the door as the police officers moved further into the room. Sophie took the seat vacated by the mother while Dale stood by the window, plonking himself down on the window sill.

"So, how are you feeling?" Sophie asked. Patience was not her strong point. She needed as much information as she could, and quickly, but right now she needed to build trust.

"I've been better." There was a sadness to his laughter. "I'm grateful, ya know...to be alive."

"Yeah, scary shit, right?" Sophie acknowledged. They spent a few minutes discussing his injuries and the therapy he was going to need moving forwards, but eventually Sophie shifted gear and began to ask the questions she needed answering. "So, Gary, I need to ask you a few questions now that, well...I know it's going to be difficult, but I need you to try really hard for me. We want to catch this guy...before he tries this again with someone else."

"Okay, I didn't see much though. He hit me from behind."

"Alright, well let's back up a little bit. You were going into town to meet Brian, right?"

"Yeah, we had a date planned. Dinner and then a movie." He smiled at the thought. He really liked dating Brian. It had only been only a few months, but that wasn't the point. "I stopped off at the Duke and grabbed a couple of drinks. I was early and well, things have been a bit stressful recently, and I didn't want to arrive all worked up. So, I stopped off and relaxed a little bit."

Sophie nodded. "And you always take the cut through along the towpath?"

"Yeah, it's the quickest way."

Sophie nodded again at the simple answer. "Yeah it is." She smiled reassuringly. "Okay, so you've turned off the bridge and you're on the towpath...what do you see?"

Gary closed his eyes and thought about it. The path wasn't wide. If you passed anyone then one of you would need to step aside onto the grass. The river was to the right of him as he walked, bushes and trees to the left. "There was a woman, she was jogging and pushing a pushchair, coming towards me." Sophie looked back towards Dale and made sure he was taking notes; he was. "I remember walking a little further along and I heard...like a kid screaming, not bad screaming, but having fun, ya know?"

"Yeah."

"And I turned around...I dunno why, but I did, I turned around to see where it came from and then..." He stopped for a moment, stared out towards the window. "I felt this almighty pain in the back of my head. I don't even remember hitting the ground." His eyes watered, but he held back the tears – for now. Sophie reached over and picked up the box of hospital-issue tissues from the table that hovered above the bed. Gary took them and placed them into his lap with a thank you. "When I woke up...he had dragged me into the bushes. Once he realised I was awake he started punching me."

"Did he say anything?"

"Yes, he kept saying that I should have 'told the truth.' Over and over."

"The truth? He didn't say what that meant?"

Gary shook his head. "No, I don't think so...I said I didn't know what I was supposed to have done." He pulled a tissue out of the box and dabbed at his eyes. "But, he just kept hitting me and I blacked out again...next thing I woke up and my hand...he glued my hands, what kind of freak does that?" He cried out and the door opened in an instant as his parents checked to see if he was ok. Sophie held up a palm and they backed out. "I'm sorry, it's all just so..."

"It's fine, you have every right to be upset, Gary." She reached out a hand and touched his arm. "You want to take a break?"

"No, no I'll be okay."

"You're very brave."

"I dunno about that, Brian says I'm a baby when it comes to anything scary." He smiled weakly.

"Me too," Dale admitted, his boyish grin making Gary blush.

"He poured something down my throat. Squeezed my cheeks to open my mouth and just...he tipped the bottle and it poured all over me. I was choking."

"Vodka, from the bottle he then glued to your hands," Sophie explained. She was sure if he thought about it that he probably already knew the answer to that, but memories would do a funny thing when you were traumatised. "Did you see what he looked like?" She continued, bringing them all back to the point in hand.

"Not really, I was groggy...out of it. It was like I was drunk or I dunno...my focus was off. He had this cap on, a football cap." He still didn't understand just how much vodka had been poured down his throat. Sophie moved on.

"Okay, what colour?"

"It was Woodington Athletic, blue with the white motif." He winced as his lip pinched. "Brian is a fan."

"That's brilliant Gary, really helpful. Anything else about him that you can remember?"

"He had blonde hair."

Chapter Fifteen

They wished Gary well and left the room, passing the parents and now the boyfriend too. Sophie raked both hands through her hair and looked at Saint. He opened his mouth as if to speak, and then thought better of it when the mother moved towards them.

"You make sure you catch this bastard," she hissed. In her seventies, she didn't look as though she took too many prisoners though.

"We will do everything we can," Dale replied. "We want this bastard just as much as you do."

~Doll~

"What the fuck? Blonde?" She patted her pockets for her cigarettes. "We need to get over to the lab and find out if there is any mistake with that hair colour! Nothing about this makes any sense." She took off along the corridor, only to almost stop in her tracks when she saw Rachel up ahead at the nurses' station. They hadn't spoken since their night together. Something flipped her insides as the nurse turned and focused her gaze on her. The appraising way in which her eyes travelled down the lean body of the detective before gliding back up and settling on her face was as erotic as anything Sophie had ever witnessed, and she felt it like a lightning bolt straight to her core.

There was a subtle nod from Sophie as they passed. Dale waved at Becky, grinning like an idiot and oblivious. If she had the time then she would have stopped and said hello, but their social life would have to wait for now. She needed to speak with Tristan as soon as she could. They were searching for the wrong man!

~Doll~

Three cigarettes later and they had their answer. They had had to wait while Tristan Barnard finished off an autopsy. Choosing to stand out in the cold lighting one cigarette after another had been preferable, but eventually they had been summoned.

The hair that had been found on victim number three was 100% that of a redhead.

"There is no doubt, Detective. Call it whatever you want: redhead, ginger, strawberry blonde. It is what it is and it was found inside the eye socket and matches the lacrimal fluid. The likelihood that it belongs to anyone other than the killer is minute!"

"So, we have two killers now?" Dale asked. "It doesn't make any sense."

"It's never made sense," she said, walking away and back towards the car. "Why did he go for the hands?"

~Doll~

Sophie Whitton got home that night to find a bag packed and waiting for her. It was left on the leather sofa in the lounge, along with another bag containing her important paperwork.

"What's this?" she asked as she entered the room. Yvonne sat upright in the armchair opposite. Her face looked resigned, but she kept her gaze on her lover's face.

"You're the detective, I would have thought it obvious." She spoke calmly enough, but Sophie noted the tense twitch of her jaw indicating she was barely holding it together.

"You want me to leave?"

"I think it's for the best...we clearly have a different path to follow." She fidgeted in her seat a little and played with the button on her blouse. "I hoped that you would have made the effort the other night and come home. Jerry and Paul...It was an important conversation and I thought that we were both on the same page..."

"I *had* a victim..." Her voice raised.

"Yes, you did and I get that, I do, Sophie, but it's not enough...not for me, not anymore." Yvonne stood up and walked unsteadily across the room to where Sophie stood. The detective appeared shell-shocked. "I am going ahead with it. I've talked with Jerry and both of them are still happy to help." She cupped Sophie's face and smiled sadly. "I want a child, and I can't bring a child into a relationship with someone that cannot be there for me, let alone him or her."

"So, that's it... you've decided and I don't even get a say in it?"

"You had the chance to have a say on Saturday..." Her own voice raised now. She took a calming breath and began again. "I think it would be best that you move out for a few days and consider what you want from this; from me."

"Where am I going to go?"

~Doll~

Her hotel room was drab. Blue carpets and blue drapes. It matched her mood perfectly. There was a double bed with clean sheets and a hanging area for clothing. At least she had a kettle, several little sachets of coffee and sugar, a few teabags, and those awful little plastic pots of milk.

She paid in advance for 5 nights initially, and as she'd handed over her credit card to pay, she thought about where life was taking her. Work was everything, but did it have to be? Could she be the person Yvonne wanted her to be? Did she want to be that person? She loved Yvonne, she didn't doubt that, but was she still in love with her?

Opening the bag, she pulled out the first item of clothing, and studied it. Just a shirt – a pink, cotton button up, but it was one that Yvonne had always liked. One by one she pulled out the other clothes and hung them in the area that was supposed to be a wardrobe. She tossed her underwear into a drawer and placed the paperwork inside the hotel safe. And then she sat down on the edge of the bed. Her shoulders sagged as she looked around at her new home for the next few nights.

It felt like hours that she sat there just staring at the wall; there wasn't even a pattern to look at, just a plain blue wall. In reality it was just 30 minutes, but her brain was in overdrive. The case...Yvonne...Rachel.

~Doll~

The door opened and Rachel stepped aside silently, allowing Sophie entrance. She closed the door and locked it. Turning, she found the detective standing still in the hallway, hands pushed deep into her pockets with her long fringe falling forward, hiding half of her face. She looked lost.

Rachel hadn't been upset to wake up and find her gone that morning. She expected it, if she was honest, and would have been more surprised if she had rolled over and found her there. Women like Whitton were easy enough to read. She was intense, trying to please everyone. She needed to succeed and bring justice to those who couldn't fight for themselves, even if that meant that she lost, and right now, she looked as though she had lost.

"I was just about to have a bath," Rachel informed her. She wore a silk kimono-style bathrobe that was knotted tightly around her waist with a corresponding belt, yet it still separated to reveal her cleavage. Neither woman had moved from the hallway.

"I should have called first...." Sophie scratched her head and tried to hide her embarrassment at just assuming she would be welcome. "I should go."

Rachel studied her for a moment before walking past her and further into the house. "Or you could join me."

~Doll~

The bathroom was at the top of the stairs. Rachel had left the door open, and the steam was drifting out onto the landing. She was using candles; the light was soft and inviting. Just like Rachel.

Sophie leant against the door frame and surveyed the sight. Rachel was already submerged under the water of a roll-top bath that stood just away from the wall. Bubbles floated freely on the top and covered her right up to her pale and freckled shoulders. She had her hair piled up on top of her head and her hands rested easily on either side, pink nail varnish starkly bright against the white enamel. Sophie knew she could walk away right now, go home and beg Yvonne to sit down, talk and work things out.

Instead she closed the door, her palm resting flat against it as it softly clicked closed, her eyes too. Shrugging her jacket off, she hung it on the hook. She kicked her shoes off at the same time as she yanked her top off over her head; she hadn't bothered with a bra, wasn't like she had much to put in one anyway. Rachel watched her, admiring the nakedness as it was revealed. Sharp hip bones and solid thighs. Whitton was an enigma that she wanted to explore.

When she was fully naked, she stepped over to the bath and waited for Rachel to sit forward. But the blonde just shook her head, chuckling.

"You're in the front." She sat up and further back, making room for Sophie to step in between her legs.

This would be a first. Sophie hadn't shared a bath with many people, but when she had, she had always sat behind. "Come on, get in. Let me take care of you." It wasn't often she just did as she was told either, or had someone so willing to just look after her well-being.

Rachel wrapped her legs around her waist and pulled her by the shoulders until she was lying back against her chest, the warm water sloshing gently against her rhythmically. "Just relax, Detective."

"Sophie." She said it quietly, as though by saying it out loud it would mean something more.

"Sorry?"

"My name, is Sophie."

"Sophie? I would not have guessed that, Detective." She smiled and wrapped her arms around Sophie's chest, tightening her hold, cushioning her against her soft, warm breasts. "Just breathe and relax."

Sophie let her head fall back and felt warm lips ghost her ear and cheek. She inhaled deeply and exhaled unhurriedly as her eyes slowly closed. They lay like that for a while, silent and comfortable.

"So, where does she think you are?" Rachel asked, surprising Sophie with her directness.

"You know about...that I'm in a relationship?"

"Of course, Becky warned me off...told me I was wasting my time..." She pressed her lips to the side of Sophie's head once more. She enjoyed the feeling of Sophie's hand sliding along her arms and holding her in place, and she would take delight in pleasuring the tough cop anytime she requested it.

"A hotel...she asked me to leave."

"Because of..."

"No, she doesn't...I didn't tell her about...this." Sophie shook her head. "I don't even know what this is."

For a moment Rachel remained silent. She relaxed back and kept her hold on the detective as they slid together further under, the water wrapping around them both. "I guess, it's whatever we want it to be. I pursued you, maybe I shouldn't have, but I've always thought that life is too short not to go after the things in life that you want. I accept though that what I want isn't always shared, and right now you can stay or go...that's up to you."

Chapter Sixteen

Curtains hung tightly closed. The room smelt of damp and was stale, even with the four air fresheners; they did nothing to cover the underlying stench of decay. The bed was unmade, no sheet, just a coverless duvet heaped in a pile on the mattress. He had climbed out of it every day and back into it every night over the last few months, but not tonight.

The room was empty of anything personal. He didn't keep his things here. The last thing he had wanted was anyone going through them, tainting them. They were his; special things that deserved to be kept away from everyone else.

He only ever brought with him a change of clothing and a razor, unless it was washing day. Then he would drag his bag into the grimy kitchen and get it all in the machine. He could come and go without anyone paying any attention to him. But, he wouldn't be sleeping there tonight, or any other night now.

Nobody on the outside took any notice of this strange family and the comings and goings in the house. At least if they did, they never said anything, or reported it to anyone, until now. As he pulled up to the kerb further along the street, he had seen the police car parked outside. He watched as two coppers snooped about. He didn't hang around, slipping the car into first and pulling away quietly. They were going to find her.

He thought about her at times. She had walked around the house as though she were a queen, and he had worshipped her at first, done everything she had asked of him and yet, it was never enough. Of course, as he had gotten older he had become less important to her. It was like déjà vu.

His nimble fingers slowly rolled the joint. He enjoyed a spliff; it relaxed him and let his mind finally switch off so that he could sleep – he had picked up the habit from his father. Holding the lighter to the end of the long, white joint, he watched as the flame took hold and burnt off the excess paper. The strong smell of marijuana wafted upwards, and he breathed it in before sucking hard on the joint and inhaling the pungent smoke deep into his lungs. His eyes fluttered shut as he lay back against the door. The backseat of the car inside his garage would have to do for now, until the old bill was finished with the house – maybe he could sneak back in at some point. He was annoyed about it though. He hadn't wanted them to find her yet. She was the last piece, and now it was all out of sync. He wasn't sure they would ever understand or work it out.

He wasn't going to worry about it though, not yet anyway.

Right now, he had more pressing things to deal with. He had completely failed in his last task, but it could wait. It was the wrong time; he had gotten too eager, too confident, and hadn't been able to accomplish what he needed to do. It was too public; he needed to be more patient. Now he had to start again, find *him* again.

And this time he wouldn't fail. He would make them all see that he was done with them all.

Chapter Seventeen

Rachel was on an early shift, and that meant an alarm call at 5:30 a.m. She smiled to herself as she reached across for the alarm and found a warm body still in bed with her. She had half expected her to climb out of the bath and leave, following the conversation, but was pleasantly surprised and very pleasantly stimulated for the better part of the night when she didn't.

Dark hair disappeared under the duvet as Sophie tried to avoid the irritating noise of the beeping alarm. It hadn't escaped her notice that for the second time in weeks, she was in no rush to get out of bed and head to work. Did that mean something? Was she that desperate to avoid things with Yvonne that she had thrown herself into the case? Maybe she was just frustrated at getting nowhere on the case and therefore resigned to just never catching him? Or was it something as simple as the blonde lying in the bed beside her?

Sophie rolled over and stared sleepily at the face across the bed. Tired green eyes looked back at her, and she felt a little guilt at keeping her awake quite so late. A slow smile worked its way to her own face as she recalled the way those eyes had sparkled and teased.

"What are you smiling about so early?" Rachel grinned back, rolling onto her side to face the woman in her bed. "Hmm, something from last night?"

"Nothing." Sophie blushed at being caught and then caught herself smiling when Rachel did. Rachel seemed to just see right through her. "What time is it?"

"A god-awful hour invented purely to torture us." She leant across and placed a kiss against Sophie's bare shoulder. "It's five-thirty. You getting up? You can stay here if you want, get another couple of hours?"

Sophie yawned and stretched. It would be so easy to roll over and fall back to sleep, but that would set a precedent she wasn't prepared for right now. It was one thing coming over and sleeping with her, but it was a whole different story to start acting like they were a couple.

"No, I'll get up. I need to go back to the hotel and get changed anyway."

"Sure. Well, I'm on a 12-hour today."

"Okay." Sophie's fringe flopped forwards as she nodded. The intensity about her came off of her in waves and washed over Rachel, drowning her, sucking her down into a current she was sure she could swim against – just.

"Hey, you can come over if you want. I'm just saying I won't be home before seven."

~Doll~

Someone had put up a Christmas tree, in the middle of fucking November! Baubles and tinsel had been placed lovingly by someone in an attempt to liven up the office. They had even made a pretend post box for Christmas cards. Clearly people had too much time on their hands, considered Whitton as she stood in front of it admiring the effort.

"Whitton? My office," Chief Inspector Adam Turner called out across the room. A series of hoots and comments about what she had done were bandied about. She gave them all a quick middle finger that attracted even more whoops of laughter.

"Yes, sir?" she said, closing the door behind her. She turned to find the senior officer already sitting at his desk.

"Take a seat," he commanded, his manner always stern. There was a lot of respect for Turner from the ranks. He had worked his way up, unlike the new influx of graduates who didn't have a clue. "Uniform received a call last night about a missing person. Unfortunately they didn't have the man power to do much more than log the call until this morning...a concerned neighbour apparently."

She fidgeted about in her seat, not quite sure where this was going or why she was being told about it. She was busy enough with the Doll Maker.

"You might want to take Saint and head over there now. Barnard is on his way, but I have told them to hold the scene until you arrive."

"Sir?"

"You'll see when you get there."

~Doll~

The house they parked in front of didn't stand out in any way other than the fact it was cordoned off with police tape warning anyone not to cross it, and the S.O.C.O. team that were in and out in their bright white coveralls.

A small patch of overgrown grass was set inside a low three-foot-high crumbling wall with only the wheelie bins for a companion. She stood outside, taking it all in, watching like a hawk at the comings and goings. A missing person had now clearly become something more serious. They flashed their warrant cards at the officer guarding the perimeter. He lifted the tape and they ducked underneath.

"The house is registered to a Gloria Armstrong. 51 years old. Record as long as your arm and mine," Dale said, reading off the clipboard he had been given by the uniformed officer. "Prostitution, fraud, kiting, every petty crime going...shoplifting, drug possession, weed, coke...you name it, she's tried it...surprised she's lived this fucking long, to be honest."

Sophie smirked and gave him a nudge. "Have some respect, Dale. What else do we know?"

"Nothing much. Says she never married, but she did have a son. A Gregory Armstrong."

"Right, well we need to find him, make sure he is aware of his mother's demise." She looked around for anyone who would know where to go next. "Oi, where's the show?" she called out to a stumpy little woman in uniform.

"Front room, on the left as you go in. You might wanna...ya know, cover ya nose."

"That bad?" Dale said.

"Not the worst, but the room's been closed up for a while, and ya know how decay stinks up the place." They both nodded a thanks at her and continued up the two steps that led into the house. The house was long past being cared for. What was left of the wallpaper was hanging off the wall, probably from the 70s judging by the brown tones. The carpets were threadbare and filthy. You could smell the stench from the hall, like rotting meat and iron.

"Ah, Detectives!" Tristan Barnard's voice boomed out from their left. "Just who we were waiting for...get a load of this." He moved aside and made room for them. In the center of the room was a chair, an old wooden carver that had seen better days, and strapped to it was the skeletonized figure of who they all assumed was Gloria Armstrong. Her wrists had been strapped to the arms of the chair with belts. The ties hung loosely now that the skin had dried out and tightened around the bones; same with the ankles. A big stain on the carpet where the bodily fluids had leaked and dried was evident on the floor around the chair. "You'll notice if you look more closely that the victim has similar post mortem wounds to our other victims. The mouth has been sewn shut. The ears were removed. *And* although one would expect the eyeballs to be missing on a corpse of this nature, I am pretty sure when I get her on the table and investigate that I'll find they were removed forcibly and not eaten away by insects." He stood aside and poked at the head. "Oh, and there is this." One of his minions held up a clear plastic evidence bag containing a doll.

"How long she been here?" Dale inquired as he looked around the room. His nose wrinkled at the foul stench that lingered still.

"I would estimate it at 8 months judging by the state of the body...and the date on the newspaper." Barnard smiled and pointed towards the folded paper on the table, already placed inside a clear forensic bag. The headline glared in black and white, 'Lady Fenwick dies suddenly in freak accident.' Whitton smirked back at the pathologist. "Hardly a lady here, if I dare judge."

"So, this is the first one," Sophie stated rather than asked.

"Looks that way," Barnard agreed.

Leaving the forensic team to get on with what they needed to do, Whitton and Saint moved out of the room and began to explore the rest of the house. Uniform had already searched the place for anybody else and found the house empty, but that didn't mean there wasn't something else to find.

"This is getting weirder every day. We get three young blonde women, then an older man and now...this?" Saint's confusion was written all over his pale face, but Whitton agreed; this was turning weirder.

"You take the kitchen and any other space you find on this level. I'll go over upstairs." Whitton was already halfway up the stairs while she gave her instructions, pulling on her gloves. The stairs creaked and reminded her of Rachel's place, only this house was nothing like the lovely home she had just left.

There were no pictures on the wall, not even a stain where one had once hung. The landing held four doors. She opened the first and stepped into the room that was directly above the one where Gloria Armstrong met her end. A single bed with a stained mattress atop it. No bedding other than a bunched up duvet. There was a walnut wardrobe and a matching chest of drawers, both empty and covered in dust. There were the remnants of old posters on the walls and an action man with one leg missing. If anyone had lived here, then it was under very basic conditions. There was a strange smell to the room: the sweetness of decay, the mustiness of rot, and the overwhelming stink of air-fresheners; four hung off the wardrobe door knobs.

Moving on to the next door, she found an airing cupboard. A few threadbare sheets and some old mismatched towels were inside. She lifted each one and checked for anything hidden; nothing.

Door number three was the bathroom. It smelt almost as bad as the room below. She wasn't sure if the toilet had ever been cleaned in its life, and she really didn't want to know what was in the bowl.

"Jesus, who lives in a shithole like this anyway?" she mumbled to herself. The last door led to the room that had to be Gloria's. One double bed covered in satin sheets and a lot of pillows. The wardrobe was stuffed with cheap dresses and outfits she didn't want to imagine anyone wearing. There were a lot of uniforms, mostly nurses, naughty maids, that kind of thing. She closed the door on it all and opened the top drawer on the dresser. Underwear and tights. It was in the third drawer that things got interesting: sex toys and magazines. The kind of mags that were illegal in most countries.

Chapter Eighteen

"Hey Dale?" Sophie called out into the hall, waiting until she heard the thump, thump, thump of his heavy boots pounding up the steps.

"Nothing downstairs. What did you find?" he asked, a little out of breath.

"A drawer full of filth." She lifted out one of the magazines and held it up for him.

He scrunched up his nose in an instant as his eyes flitted down to the drawer. "Hardcore porn?" There had to be at least 15 magazines in there amongst the dildos and vibrators. "Jesus, I am surprised anybody missed her enough to call it in."

"Right? This is one cold bitch. I don't even wanna touch the place." She blew a breath out. "Okay, let's take this room apart. You wanna let the S.O.C.O know?"

He was back within minutes carrying a handful of evidence bags. The fourth drawer was empty. They turned the room upside down. Every item of clothing was shaken and examined, bagged and tagged, but they came up with nothing else.

"If you were into this kind of crap, would you leave it where it could be found?" she asked Dale. They were going to have one of their conversations where Dale batted back ideas.

"No, I'd have a hiding place."

"Right, so why is this not hidden?" she asked, looking around the room. She was missing something.

"Maybe she was just an arrogant bitch that didn't think she would get caught?"

"Yeah, could be, but it doesn't feel right. There's more, somewhere hidden." She lifted the mattress again and flipped it off the bed completely. Nothing. "What's that?" She squinted and bent down by the dresser to examine the floor. It was an old heavy thing, and yet there were scratches on the floorboards under it. Lots of scratches. This was moved, often. "Gimme a hand, will ya?" She pushed at the end of it and shoved hard.

~Doll~

Chief Inspector Turner headed the table. Whitton and Saint faced each other on either side of him. The box on the table sat between them all like a morbid package that nobody had wanted to look through.

It was just an old shoe box - ironically a kid's shoe box; size 4 trainers. It had been wedged in between the joists under a loose floorboard.

"She had a child, a boy by the name of Gregory. Born 12th February 1987. We found one photograph on file from a stint in child protective services. He appears to be the kid in these photographs," Sophie explained, indicating the box and its contents.

"Poor little bastard," Dale muttered, shaking his head. He had had the unfortunate job of having to look through them. He would go home and hug his kids a little longer tonight.

"What is striking is that Gregory Armstrong is a redhead. Doc has confirmed that the body is that of Gloria Armstrong, Gregory's mother."

"So, we have our man?" Turner asked, his attention completely on Whitton as he passed her a cup of coffee.

"I think we do...I really think we have something. We're waiting for the doc to confirm the hair found on Sandra Bancroft is related to Gloria. However, at present we can't find him. Gregory Armstrong doesn't seem to exist anymore."

Turner looked between the pair of them and waited for further information. His ruddy face was flushing; she wasn't sure if it was the heat in here or if he was just pissed off.

"He attended school on and off, spent time in and out of the care system, and then he just disappears," Dale continued, reading from his notes.

"No college, no job...he didn't even sign on," Sophie added. "So, we've got nothing."

"What we have is a serial killer with a name and a face, of sorts," Turner said. "Get on to facial rec and have them see if they can age this kid and then find this bastard before he does any more damage."

"Yes sir."

~Doll~

Whitton had been sitting outside of the cottage for the last 45 minutes. It was a pretty little place, nothing like the filth-ridden cesspit she had spent much of the day in. There were plants lining the pathway; during the summer months they would bloom and flower, the bright colours cheerful and optimistic of sunny days.

She had watched as Rachel returned home 38 minutes ago, letting herself in without a backward glance at the car parked across the road. Sophie appreciated her figure, the way she held herself and walked confidently. Like Yvonne, she was a woman who knew exactly what she wanted from life.

She hadn't heard from Yvonne at all. Not that she really expected to. She had made it clear how she felt and what was important to her now; it didn't include Sophie while she was still a cop.

She had realised when they found the box of photographs that she couldn't be a part of bringing a child into this world if she couldn't spend her life fighting for other people's children.

She saw the way it affected Dale, how his face crumpled and his eyes saddened, and this wasn't one of his kids; his kids were safe at home, loved and cherished, not like the poor kid Gregory Armstrong was.

She lived in the darkness, walked the pathways of the shadows and lingered in the depths searching out the scum and filth of the Earth to keep families safe. She didn't know how to be anyone else. She didn't *want* to be anyone else.

Yvonne didn't understand it, and she was grateful for that, glad that her only arc into darkness came from living with the detective. She was right to walk away from that, to bring a life into a world full of light and love instead.

She could see Rachel through the window. She hadn't closed the curtains yet and the lights were on, meaning Sophie had a clear view of her silhouette. She watched her move around the room, exhausted and weary from a day dealing with people dying, in pain. As a nurse, she lived a life in the shadows too, dealing with the unkindness in the world. Rachel lived in Whitton's world.

And here she was waiting outside, ready to go in and dump her day on her.

The difference between Yvonne and Rachel, however, was night and day. Rachel got it! She understood the darkness and the exhaustion, chasing the cure. She understood the late nights and the endless fight for one thing: hope.

Chapter Nineteen

Sophie entered the cottage this time with a surety she hadn't felt before. The moment the door opened, she found her hands lifting to palm her lover's cheeks. Their lips meeting in an all-encompassing kiss. When they broke apart Sophie whispered, "It's my turn to take care of you."

Rachel found herself lifted, her legs wrapped snugly around the detective's waist as she was carried, still kissing, to the bedroom. The serious and often surly, broody and intense detective was now just Sophie, an equally intense lover, intent on completing the task at hand.

It was no surprise to Rachel that Sophie was a gentle lover, though she was completely aware that when the need arose, her detective would take control, and that intensity would show its face in other ways that were just as pleasurable. But this Sophie was a welcome diversion tonight.

She had been placed carefully back onto her feet, her clothing removed with a deftness she didn't think Sophie would possess, and now she was lying on her front with the detective's fingers pressing into her flesh, massaging the stress of the day away. The sweet scent of almond oil wafted gently, surrounding her sense with calmness. "Fall asleep if you need to," Sophie had suggested, and she was considering that option as her muscles relaxed. The problem was that her arousal had been awoken.

"I don't want to sleep," Rachel said as she twisted around. "Not while I have your attention."

Sophie grinned down at Rachel, whose blonde hair was fanned out on the pillow. Her lip gloss long gone from her pouty kiss-swollen lips.

~Doll~

Rachel was woken by the sound of movement coming from downstairs. Sophie was no longer in the bed. Sitting up, she listened. She hadn't heard the front door close, so she hadn't left.

Tip-toeing down the stairs, she could hear the clinking sound of mugs. Sophie stood at the sink wearing just a shirt, washing up. "What are you doing?" Rachel asked, her voice filled with mirth and sleep as she propped herself against the door frame.

"Fuck, don't creep up on me like that," Sophie gasped with a quick head turn in Rachel's direction before getting back to her task. "What does it look like I am doing?"

"Did I not wear you out enough?" Rachel chuckled. Moving into the room, she stepped up behind Sophie and wrapped her arms around her waist, yawning as she rested her cheek against a boney shoulder blade.

Sophie smiled, dropping the sponge into the water. "I have no complaints on that front...just got stuff on my mind that I can't switch off." She dried her hands off on the towel and turned into the embrace.

"Wanna talk about it?"

"It's late, you should go back to sleep." She stroked Rachel's cheek, noting the freckles and tracing a pathway through them.

"I'll make some cocoa while you talk." Rachel pressed her lips against Sophie's forehead. "Sit."

Tugging her shirt lower, Sophie sat on the kitchen chair, ran her fingers through her hair, and blew out a breath. "We uh...we found another body this morning." Rachel paused but didn't interrupt her. "It was pretty grim, ya know...been there a while. Anyway, it's pretty obvious that it's the mother of the man we're looking for, the Doll Maker." Now Rachel turned, two mugs of hot cocoa in her hands. She placed one down in front of Sophie and pulled another chair closer. "There was other stuff...photographs and magazines that his mother must have taken and kept." Her eyes watered and she blinked hurriedly. "I'm supposed to just..." She could feel the lump developing in her throat and tried to swallow it down. "I'm supposed to go home at night and pretend I don't see these things."

"Oh Soph, sometimes the worst part of our jobs are the things we take home with us."

Sophie wiped at her face and nodded. "This poor kid...Jesus, the things they did to him, and the world wonders why he turned out the way he did? Not that I'm justifying his actions...but..."

"I know, *we* don't all hurt people just because we have been hurt." Rachel's words were firm, and yet there was something more behind them. Sophie's eyes narrowed as she studied her face, noting the sad smile as she nodded. "My uncle..."

"Shit, I'm sorry..." Rachel placed a finger against her lips.

"Shh, it's fine...I'm okay with it now. It took a long time, but I wasn't going to let it ruin my life. I was 9 when it began and I left home as soon as I could. I was 17, emptied my bank account and packed a bag, took the first train out of town." She took Sophie's hands in her own and kissed her fingertips,

"That was brave...venturing out on your own like that. What did you do?"

"When I felt like enough miles were between me and them, I found a bedsit and enrolled in college. I always knew I wanted to be a nurse."

"So, they never came looking for you?" Sophie asked, intrigued even more now.

Rachel laughed and leant forwards, capturing lips with her own. "Enough about me. Go on, get it off your chest, what else is bothering you?"

Sophie tilted her head back and considered her words. "So, it looks like this kid is the Doll Maker..."

"But?"

"But...he is a redhead, the hair found at one of the scenes was from a redhead...Gary says the man that attacked him was a blonde." She sipped her drink and savoured the sweet liquid as it warmed her.

Rachel considered this new information while Sophie remained quiet. "It seems as though you have several options to consider. One, there are two of them?"

"I don't know. Everything is a possibility, at this point I'm not writing anything off." She took another sip.

Rachel nodded. "Two, you've got the wrong man?"

"Again, it's always possible, but everything points to him...what he did to the mother, if it is him, it fits." She winced, not wanting to go into too much more detail.

"Okay, so three, how does somebody with red hair suddenly have blonde hair?" Rachel pondered.

Sophie sipped her cocoa some more. It was delicious and sweet, with just a hint of bitter chocolate. It reminded her of being a kid. She wondered what Rachel had been like as a child, and then her thoughts had moved towards Gregory Armstrong.

"Or he dyed it, well I imagine he would have to bleach it actually," Rachel was saying, bringing her back out from her thoughts.

"That could be it. All the press reports are asking for a red-haired man. So, maybe he has just bleached his hair!" She leant forward and grasped Rachel's face in her hands, kissing her lips.

"Thank you. Sometimes I'm too busy looking for the difficult answer, when I just needed..."

"To talk it through, I know...now, bed! We both need more sleep. You can catch your killer in the morning."

Chapter Twenty

The forensic team were still at the property on Myrtle Street. Due to the find the previous day of a body and child porn, the S.O.C. Officers would tear the place apart. Floorboards would come up, plaster would be pulled off the walls, and the cavities behind would be searched. All of the furniture was lifted, opened, and subsequently moved out. Mattresses were tested for DNA. They didn't find anything more in the house. Eventually the house would be pulled down, and its macabre history nothing more than local gossip and urban myths.

The garden, however, was another story.

There was a well-worn patio of broken paving slabs, with a grid of weeds pushed up between the gaps and cracks, furious that someone had attempted to smother them. Two flowerbeds would have lined the edge of the overgrown grass had anyone cared enough to plant any. They dug it all up anyway, and found another body.

"This one has been in the ground a long time... and it's male!" Barnard exclaimed almost gleefully. Sophie blew out a disbelieving breath and rubbed her chin.

"So, it could be completely unrelated?" Dale asked as he looked into the unmarked grave. The body was pretty much a skeleton, just patches here and there of rotted flesh and hair.

"*That* is your job to discover, young Dale. What I can tell you, however, is that the body has been here for eight to twelve years.

I'd be leaning more towards eight to ten if pushed, but I'll know more later."

"The more we get into this, the weirder it gets," Dale said, looking to Sophie, who was yet to speak. "We need an ID as soon as, Doc."

"I know the rules, DS Saint. You'll have your name as soon as I have it." He turned away and continued talking to his minions.

"So, you've managed to piss off the doc, and forgotten my coffee this morning...on a roll today, Dale," Sophie quipped. "Shall we go and see if we can find anything to help us?"

"You're in a good mood. Yvonne put out last night, eh?" He laughed as she opened the driver's door to the car. When he realised that Sophie wasn't playing along, he got in. "Everything alright, Soph?"

"Everything is fine, we're just...we're having a break," she admitted, too easily.

"What? Why? You two always seemed so...put together."

She started the car and pulled her seatbelt across her chest, locking it safely into place. Checking the traffic through her side mirror, and then over her shoulder to be sure, she pulled out of the parking space.

"She wants a kid," she stated, as if it were that simple an answer.

"And?" he asked reaching forward to turn the radio off. "I thought that's what you wanted too?"

She rubbed her face and then indicated, checking the traffic as she turned into the left hand lane. "It ain't that simple though, is it?" She glanced at him quickly before putting her eyes back on the road again. "If you were doing this five years ago, before you had Ella, would you have been so eager?"

He thought about it. His kids were his world, and he couldn't imagine a world without them. But back when they decided to have kids, he was still in uniform and Becky had been a bank nurse, working when she wanted to around her studies. They were lucky too; they had Becky's mum to babysit for them. "I dunno, I guess it wouldn't be quite so simple now."

"Yvonne wants me to stop doing this, get a desk job or stay at home." She glanced at him again. "I know it's selfish, but I just don't want that, and bringing a kid into this world...with all these evil bastards out there?" She shook her head sorrowfully. "She asked me to leave."

"Holy shit. You need somewhere to stay?" He was genuinely upset for her. DS Sophie Whitton, as she was known then, had been the first person to help him settle when he transferred out of uniform and became a detective. He had her back, and he knew she had his.

"Nah, I'm good, got a hotel room for now, and I'll figure something out." She had barely spent an entire night there yet, but she wasn't going to tell Dale that.

Chapter Twenty-One

It was December, and the body in the garden was anonymous for now; he hadn't been missed for many Christmases. Dr Barnard estimated him to have been in his late teens when he was beaten to death. His skull was fractured in several places around the back of the head. He had been hit by something heavy and flat, like a cricket bat. He hadn't seen it coming, as there were no defensive fractures. He had been hit on the back of the head and the back of the left shoulder blade, and his pelvis was cracked. It was vicious and had given the victim no chance of survival.

They were waiting for a dental match, but that could take weeks, if not longer, though they had placed a rush on it. Therefore the first thing they did was search all missing person records and collect a database of potential names. They then would have to hunt down the dental records of all and any who were registered with a dentist and then check the x-rays of the victim against them and hope to God that they found a match.

"We've got 56 names so far, all within the 8 to 12 year time frame of being missing, and all within the parameters of 18 to 25 years of age. We just have to hope this person is in a system somewhere." There were coffees on the table between them, going undrunk as Sophie explained where they were on the case.

"I know the frustration is getting to us all Sophie. We can only do what we can do. When was the last time you took a day off?" Chief Inspector Adam Turner sat back in his chair and studied her.

For a tall woman, she looked remarkably small as she shrunk down into the chair. Thin and wiry, she looked haunted.

"I dunno, sir."

"Well, maybe the rest of today and tomorrow will be a good time to recharge?" he suggested, his eyes fixed and daring her to argue.

"But..."

"There is nothing happening right now that Branson and Saint can't deal with. If anything breaks I will personally call you back in, but I can't afford to have Health & Safety, or HR, or the bloody union on my back because you're working more hours than the law allows." He smiled warmly at her. "Go home and take a break, the world will keep turning."

~Doll~

Walking into the home she shared with Yvonne, she was amazed at how little she had missed it these past weeks or so. She dropped her keys down on the shelf just inside the doorway and kicked off her shoes. It was warm, as usual, and she shrugged off her jacket to hang it on the hook. She could smell Yvonne's perfume as it permeated the air around her, a little nudge at her memories.

Everything in its place and a place for everything. Entering the kitchen, she took in the small table that had seen its fair share of entertainment. The first few months and even year of their relationship and living together hadn't been like they were now.

They had made love on that table, several times. Celebrated promotions and birthdays. Argued, screamed and shouted at each other. They'd cooked together and laughed at Sophie's silly jokes, and entertained their friends, but that was all a long time ago.

There was no point in reminiscing now. That wasn't why she was here. She flicked on the stereo, found a local radio station playing something upbeat, and got on with the task at hand.

The bedroom didn't look any different. She knew where to find the suitcases and bags they used whenever they travelled abroad. She took her time, removing each item from the wardrobe, folding and placing it neatly into the case. By the time she was finished, she had three cases and a bag.

Sophie didn't hear the door open and close or notice Yvonne standing in the doorway of the room until she spoke. "So, I see you've come to a decision then?" She pressed her lips together and nodded to herself as though answering a question only she had heard. She had, after all, started this ball rolling; she shouldn't be surprised that Sophie would make any decision swiftly.

"Hi." Sophie finished zipping up the bag and stood uncertainly on the other side of the room. "I figured it was best to just..." She sighed heavily. "You're right. I live in the darkness, and that's no place for a child."

"I love you Sophie, and if there was any other compromise, I'd find it." Yvonne gulped and blinked away the tears before smiling sadly. "I'll buy you out...of the flat I mean, I'll make sure you get a fair deal and..."

"I know, I'm not worried about that. I love you too Von, but you know you need to live the life you want, and I can't give you that. If there is one thing this job has shown me, it's that life is way too short." Sophie moved around the bed and stood in front of Yvonne. Her lover for the last four years was openly weeping now. "Hey, come on. It's going to be okay. This has been coming, if we're honest, right?" Her arms wrapped around Yvonne so naturally. She felt Yvonne nod against her chest; it was for the best. It was what they needed to do, what Yvonne needed her to do.

Before she had time to think, they were kissing, their lips parting and inviting the other in, frantically swallowing one another's fears. Her fingers slid easily from around Yvonne's waist to slide upwards and into her hair to pull her in close. It took Sophie seconds to press Yvonne against the wall, using her weight to hold her in place as her hands now moved lower, tugging her skirt up, high enough that she could part her thighs and slip her hand between them, her underwear no match for the frantic need to love each other one last time.

It would be the last time Sophie looked at these walls, the last time she lay in this bed, and the last time she worshipped this body writhing beneath her.

~Doll~

The last time Sophie had had a drink was months ago at a party she had attended with Yvonne. It was a work do that Yvonne needed to attend and impress the higher-ups; it had worked too, when she was offered her second promotion of the year. Sophie had been drinking champagne cocktails that day. Tonight, it was just pints of lager with whisky chasers. She was on her fourth already. Or was it her fifth? She hadn't been counting.

They had lain in bed for an hour just holding one another before Yvonne asked her to leave. They cried some more and hugged at the door. Yvonne helped her to carry her bags to the car, and they held one another one last time before Sophie climbed into the vehicle and with teary eyes, drove away.

Dumping everything back at the hotel, she made arrangements for another week's stay and then called a cab to take her to a bar she knew. It was the bar all emergency service personal seemed to be drawn to, as it was walking distance from the police station, hospital, and fire station, but she didn't see any of C.I.D in there. Grateful for that fact, she sat at the bar and ordered her drinks.

"Want another?" the guy behind the bar asked, noticing her glass was almost empty. Nice-looking guy with a shaved head and a crooked smile. His voice didn't match the image though. Posh boy dumbing down.

"Yeah, why not?" she slurred a little, though she wasn't drunk – yet.

"You don't come in here often, huh?" he stated, making small talk as he poured her lager. She looked at him and studied his features as he continued to smile, and she concluded that he was a bit of a dick.

"I'm normally too busy." She sneered. She wasn't here for polite chit chat.

"Oh, and what is it that keeps a hot chick like you so busy?" He placed her pint down in front of her and leant his elbows on the bar, on the edge of being just that little bit too close to her personal space.

Hot chick? Who was he kidding? Firstly, she looked like shit. A lack of sleep mixed with the fact she had red-rimmed eyes from crying all afternoon wasn't a good look. Secondly, she looked gay as fuck, so yeah, she might be a hot chick to another hot chick, but that was about it. And thirdly, she was at least 10 years older than him. He was cute though; shaved head and freckles. He seemed sure of himself, which she assumed was just as much of an attraction to straight women as it was to lesbians! Though there was an arrogance to his confidence that wasn't quite so enticing.

"Barking up the wrong tree, mate," she said, wrapping her hand around the glass and enjoying the cold condensation as she lifted it to her lips and took a swig. He looked confused; his smile had slipped a little as he continued to stare. "I fuck women," she said, making it clear.

"Oh, you're...you're gay! Okay, I just figured, ya know, it was...ya know the image... I guessed it was just fitting in at work."

"Fitting in at work? Fuck, work's the only place I do fit." She laughed ironically. He smiled, a little unsure of her now as he looked up at the next customer. "And anyway, I am way too old for you," she added quickly.

"I like an older woman; experience has a lot to offer." He winked with a grin as she shook her head at him and smirked.

"What can I get ya?" he grinned at the latest customer. There was always another pretty face he could try and chat up. The woman that had stepped up to the bar behind the copper wasn't interested in him either. Her long slender neck was hidden under a black roll neck sweater, black jeans ripped at the knees, exposing flesh. The long leather coat was unbuttoned, and she had one hand in her jeans pocket. But she only had eyes for the dark-haired miserable cop.

"I'll have a gin and orange, thank you." She sat down in the seat next to Sophie. "Detective, you ready for another?"

Sophie twisted around in her seat to find Rachel sitting there smiling at her. "Are you following me?"

"I think someone has delusions of grandeur, no? As it happens, I usually drop in here on a Thursday evening, if my shift allows. Sometimes it's nice to just be around people...people that don't require me to wipe their arse or clean up their puke, ya know?" The barman placed a tall glass in front of her. Gin over ice and filled with juice. She thanked him and handed over a tenner. "You okay?"

"Yeah."

"How many have you had?"

"Does it matter?" she slurred, swigging down another mouthful.

"Well, if I am going to catch up..." She grinned and reached out a hand to caress her face. Sophie turned her cheek away and took another gulp. "What's wrong?"

"Nothing. Just getting drunk."

"I see." Rachel took a mouthful of her own drink and got up from her seat. If her feelings were hurt, she did a great job of hiding it. "Well, I'll be sitting over there if you decide you want some company." She pointed across the room to a small table by the window, but Sophie didn't bother to look up.

Rachel watched the sullen detective order another drink and stare off into space, her mind clearly occupied with something distressing. Rachel sipped her gin, the ice clinking in the glass as she swirled it. She would give Sophie her space to work through things.

"Hi, Rachel." A voice from her right disturbed her from her own thoughts. She looked up to find Pete standing next to the table, hovering awkwardly as he waited for her to reply.

"Oh hey Pete, you okay?" She smiled at the shy young man. Pete the Porter they all called him, although there were a few that called him Pervy Pete, which she thought was a little unfair as he had never done anything to deserve it that she knew of. He was just shy and awkward from what she could tell.

"Yeah, I'm good." He fidgeted from one foot to the other as she waited for him to continue. "So, uh...can I...d'ya want another drink?" he finally got out. She looked at her glass, almost empty. The object of her attention was still brooding by herself at the bar.

"Sure, why not?" She grinned as his face lit up with surprise.

"Oh, okay...uh?"

"Gin and orange, thank you." She held the empty glass up for him, and he took it. He moved like lightning towards the bar; still grinning. She took the opportunity to check her phone for any messages. Just the one from a colleague wanting to swap shifts. So, she replied back and settled against the bench to watch Sophie.

It wasn't like her to chase after someone as brazenly as she had with the detective. Usually she would make her interest clear and let them make the decision to follow it up, but with Sophie, there was just something about the detective that made her want more.

Her life up until this point had been somewhat unhappy, she could admit that. Her father just hadn't been there for them. Her mother had made excuses, and only seemed happy when she was with him. It was sad, really. Of course, when her uncle had taken an interest in her and begun to touch her, she found she was on her own. The new baby was taking up all of her mother's time, and her father had taken even less of an interest in them all.

As soon as she turned seventeen, she had been able to persuade her mother to hand over the bank account that held her inheritance from her grandparents. It wasn't a huge sum in the grand scheme of things, but it had meant she could run, change her name and start living the life she wanted to. It had cost her, though.

The name change was simple and essential, and she hadn't looked back since. Enrolling in college and starting her nursing career had been the best thing she had ever done, and she was proud of herself. But, she had no-one to call family, no support system like other people had.

Pete reappeared holding two glasses. He stood nervously as he waited for Rachel to notice him. "Aw, thanks Pete."

He nodded and placed the drinks down on top of the coasters that were haphazardly tossed across the table. "You're welcome." He smiled and sat down opposite her. "I told him not too much ice. Nothing worse than a watered-down drink."

"Indeed, who wants that?" She smiled back at him, one eye on the figure hunched at the bar. "So, how's ya day been, Pete?"

~Doll~

Needing a cigarette, Sophie silently berated the laws of the land that now banned smoking inside a pub. She lowered a foot and found purchase on the sticky floor, holding onto the bar as she lowered her other foot down and stood unsteadily on her feet. Looking over in the direction Rachel had last been, she could see she had company: the porter guy from the hospital. Shrugging to herself, she patted down her jacket until she located her cigarettes, and then she staggered outside and lit up.

Her shoulders landed against the wall as she sucked on the cigarette and blew the smoke out into the cold night air. For once it wasn't raining, or worse still, snowing. But it was cold, and she shoved her other hand inside her jacket pocket and hunched around herself. The door to the bar opened, and another reveler staggered out into the cold and headed off to what she assumed was home.

"You left your phone on the bar," Rachel said, Sophie was amazed at just how often and easily the nurse could appear without her noticing. Her guard was down around this woman, and she didn't know why.

"Ah, thanks." She pulled her hand from her jacket and took the small item from Rachel, pushing it back into her pocket.

"No   problem,   I'm..."

"You're gorgeous." Sophie finished her sentence for her before she took a drag on her cigarette and squinted at the nurse though drunken eyes. "God, I wish things...different ya know...is all just...fucked up!" She was rambling. Being drunk would do that to you.

Chapter Twenty-Two

Floating on a cloud of softness as her head thumped to a beat of nausea, Sophie woke to a darkened room. Lifting her head wasn't a good plan, and neither was opening her eyes, so she was reliant on her other senses.

Whitney Houston crooned from a distance. The scent of Gucci lingered on the pillows, though the body that had warmed the space had long since moved; the sheets were cold against her fingertips. She groaned internally. Ending up in Rachel's bed again hadn't been her plan.

Searching her mind for the remnants of the previous night, she struggled to find the memories she needed. The last thing she remembered was smoking a cigarette...and Rachel. She winced as she recalled telling Rachel she was gorgeous, which wasn't a lie. There was something so subtle in the sexiness about her that it intrigued Whitton, but she hadn't intended to behave like a love-struck teenager and fawn all over her.

"Good morning." Rachel stood by the side of the bed holding a tray. Sophie opened one eye and groaned again, much to the blonde's amusement. "I assume you're feeling as bad as you look?" She placed the tray down on the bedside table, pushing aside the digital alarm clock.

"I...What did I drink?" she mumbled. Rachel chuckled and sat down on the edge of the bed and ran her fingers through Sophie's hair.

"I think it was lager and whisky, but how many? I have no idea." She lifted a mug of coffee from the tray for herself and took a sip. "I managed to get you home and into bed, whereupon you promptly fell asleep."

Sophie lifted the cover slightly and noted her nakedness.

"I managed to undress you also, figured you wouldn't want to sleep in your clothes." The silence lingered between them. "We didn't have sex."

Sophie groaned, then wriggled and flung the duvet off. It was a "ripping the plaster off" moment as she forced herself to sit up and pushed down the urge to vomit when her brain shook violently in the small cavity that housed it. A wave of nausea passed once more as she focused her eyes on the wall ahead until everything stopped moving.

"So, I made some toast and coffee. I figured you'd need these too." Rachel held out her hand and dropped two tablets into Sophie's palm. "When you want to talk, I'll be downstairs." She stood up and smiled down at her.

The shower helped. Her mind fog cleared a little, but that was probably down to the paracetamol more than anything else. By the time she was dressed, she felt almost human again.

She found Rachel in the living room with her feet up on the sofa reading a magazine. The headline read, 'My husband left me for another man.' She looked up as Sophie entered the room and pulled her knees up to make space for the detective. She had her hair tied back, her green eyes settled on Sophie as she placed the magazine down.

"Feeling any better?" she asked. Sophie nodded and took a seat. "Good," Rachel added with a smile as she placed her legs on top of Sophie's lap. She picked up her magazine again and continued to read.

The silence wasn't awkward. In fact, Sophie realised that she enjoyed it. Just being able to sit alongside somebody and not have to engage in a conversation to justify being there was somewhat acceptable. Yvonne had always wanted to talk. Silence meant an argument had been had. Talking was what people did at the end of the day. Finding out about each other's days and how things were going, only Yvonne didn't want to hear about Sophie's day or how things were going. So, Sophie had learnt to filter and avoid. She had learnt to come home and smile and nod in all the right places, and the silence had become a weight of all that was unsaid.

She let her head fall back against the couch and closed her eyes. She opened them to find Rachel looking at her. "I left her."

Rachel didn't speak. She had no need to.

"Officially...I moved all of my stuff out yesterday...we made love and for a moment I thought, I thought maybe that it would work...and then she asked me to leave and it's all so fucking amicable that I just...and I'm here again, waking up in your bed and I don't feel bad about it." She placed both her palms on Rachel's shins and rubbed her thumbs back and forth.

Rachel licked her lip before speaking, the magazine placed in her lap once more. "I'm not sorry that you're here either."

"Not now, but maybe you will be." She smiled sadly. "I'm rebounding..."

"I don't recall putting any stipulations on this, *Detective*. It is what it is and it lasts for as long as it lasts." Her movement was slow as she dropped the unwanted mag to the floor and clambered across to straddle Whitton's lap. "I'm a big girl, but I know what I want, Sophie, and when I don't want it anymore, then I'll be sure to let you know."

Chapter Twenty-Three

The Christmas tree had been added to over the weekend. Now the office was bedecked with garlands and tinsel. Even a fairy had found its way to the top of the tree. But any Christmas cheer had gone out of the window the second Branson had taken the call.

A concerned citizen had called it in. A white Ford Focus was ablaze out at the old brickworks. There was nothing left of it. The plate that held all of the car's information had been removed or melted in the heat. It was now nothing more than a mangled and charred frame.

Crime scene techs worked the scene regardless, searching for anything that might lead to a clue. Footprints and cigarette butts, crisp packets and broken beer bottles were all collected and logged. It looked like the kind of area that kids hung around in at night. Someone had built a fire pit and surrounded it with bigger rocks that clearly provided a seating area for eight.

"Waste of fucking time," Sophie snarled as she took in the scene and watched the men in white suits picking up the detritus.

"What is?" Dale Saint asked, his eyes glued to the burnt-out wreck.

"All of this. He is too smart to have left anything behind. Probably carries a fucking broom with him and sweeps his fucking footprints away!"

Dale chuckled at her.

"I'm out of here. Let me know if they find anything." She laughed sardonically and turned away.

~Doll~

The afternoon found Whitton in the office watching the snow fall outside of the window to her left. It wasn't laying thankfully, but the temperature had plummeted earlier in the day. She yawned and stretched her arms above her head as she contemplated the case. When the phone rang, it made her jump and she almost fell backwards off of her chair.

"Whitton." Her voice was harsh as she righted herself.

"DI Whitton, just the woman," Barnard's voice sang out. "I was hoping I'd catch you. I think I have found the identity of our skeleton."

She felt her stomach clench as the new lead surfaced and swam excitedly around her head. Of course, it didn't mean it was linked to the Doll Maker. It could easily be just a morbid coincidence, but it was something, and something was better than watching the snow flitter down.

~Doll~

Tristan Barnard sat at his desk in his pristine office reviewing his case notes. His dark brown suit was impeccable as always. He flicked his hand through his hair and smiled as he stood to greet Whitton.

"Good to see you again Detective, no Saint?" He gestured for her to take a seat.

"No sir, just me today I am afraid." She smiled; she liked the man, respected him and his point of view, and enjoyed the way he teased Dale at every opportunity. He had never let her down with evidence or his backing her during an investigation.

"It's always a pleasure." He shuffled some paperwork around on his desk before looking up at her again. Like a coiled spring, she sat on the edge of her chair, notebook in hand. He took a certain amount of enjoyment in observing the pensive detective; she intrigued him with her dedication and intense need for justice, and he couldn't deny that the entire package somewhat attracted him. "Right, so down to business. Our body belonged to a William Peter Wilson."

"Right." She wrote the name down in her notebook.

"Date of birth 15th of October 1988 in Long Horton, to a Melody Wilson aged just 15." Sophie didn't look up from her task, adding the details accurately. "He went into the care system at age three and bounced around in foster care for a while before finally settling with a Mr & Mrs..." His finger moved slowly across his paperwork until he found the name he was looking for. "Franklin. Yes, Roy and Clara Franklin"

"Okay, that's great. Have they been informed?"

"I am not aware of that." He looked up. "It would seem that dear William was a runaway, back and forth until eventually the

Franklins said enough and he was returned to the care system via St. Mildred's Home for Wayward Teenagers."

"Okay." She added those new details underneath everything else, underlining the Franklins and St Mildred's as important. When nothing further came from the doc, she looked up and found him waiting for her to finish. He pulled his glasses off before dropping his next bombshell.

"My issue, however, isn't who the body belongs to. It's the fact that he appears not to be dead." He pulled a piece of paper free from the bundle and slid it across the desk. His long fingers swiveled the image of an upside-down driver's license around to face her.

"I know him."

Chapter Twenty-Four

The room was buzzing with activity. You could feel the electricity as it passed from one member of the team to the next, the anticipation of what was to come.

Sophie had called Dale on the way in and instructed him to let Branson know. You could feel the tension; it was palpable as every officer attacked their keyboards for information. Phones were ringing and conversations were taking place as every member of the team made it their business to find every single piece of evidence and information they could on Peter William Wilson. The hospital porter had used the identity of William Peter Wilson and simply switched the Christian names around. Now they needed to locate him.

"I want warrants for his home, work, and every other known place he has even a gnat's fart of a connection to," she called out to Saint. He raised a thumb, phone held tightly against his ear.

It wouldn't take much to find a magistrate willing to issue every warrant Whitton asked for, so she was on tenterhooks and chewing her nail as she paced the floor waiting for another thumbs up from Saint so they could get moving.

She was angry with herself that he had managed to just walk about so blasé and nobody had noticed. The quiet oddball with *bleached* blonde hair.

"Got it!" Dale shouted. She grabbed her keys and was moving towards him. Stopping off at their lockers, they grabbed their handcuffs and pulled on their police-issue stab vests. It was a precaution for a threat they hoped would not come to fruition.

"Let's go. Home address first." Taking two steps at a time, they both moved in synch.

"Okay, I've got S.O.C.O. on their way. Barnard said he would meet us." It was cold outside, the kind of cold that brought a harsh sting to your cheeks and iced your veins. Dale pulled his coat tighter as he climbed into the passenger seat. He always liked to drive, but he knew there was no way Whitton was going to give up the driver's seat on this one. He glanced across at her and noted the steely look in her eyes. Her face looked pinched and tight, from the cold mainly, but also from a determination to find justice.

The traffic was light. The weather kept most people off of the roads and tucked away inside their comfortable, warm homes. However, the snowfall and falling temperatures also meant that Whitton couldn't drive at the speed she would have liked to. Instead she kept to a steady 30 mph where she could weave in and out of traffic when the opportunity arose.

~Doll~

They knocked politely once, and when no answer came, Whitton gave the order to break the door down and gain entry. It was dark and cold inside too. Using a torch as they moved around the small flat, Saint repeatedly informed any potential occupants that it was the police. It became apparent pretty quickly that nobody was at home.

The living room was small. A secondhand leather couch that had seen better days was the biggest item of furniture. A small TV sat on a battered pine stand, the focal point in the room. There was a table with two mismatched chairs and a withered pot plant that hankered for some light on top of it. The curtains were drawn; no nets or blinds. No lampshade, just a bare lightbulb. He had several books lined neatly on a shelf. Whitton tilted her head and read some of the titles; all murder and intrigue, true life crimes and fiction.

Nothing about the room suggested psychopath, but she knew that didn't necessarily make much difference. Psychopaths blended in, chameleon-like in their approach. It was only once you spent time with one that you realised just how detached from the rest of the world they were.

She left Saint to orchestrate with Barnard while she wandered through the flat and into the bedroom. There was an unmade bed with filthy unwashed sheets against the back wall, and old wardrobe with one door hanging off and a chest that didn't match. There was nothing much else.

"Dale, I am gonna head over to the hospital, see if we can pick him up there. I'll take Jeff, you stay here and let me know the minute there's anything I need to know."

"Sure Soph," he acknowledged quickly before turning his attention to one of Barnard's minions.

~Doll~

It was late in the day already, and she hoped there would still be a member of staff available to help. Jeff was almost running to keep up with her, long strides carrying her through the hospital corridors until they found the HR Department. She didn't bother with knocking.

"DI Whitton and DC Branson." She flashed her warrant card and looked towards Jeff as he did the same and dropped a copy of the warrant on her desk. "I want everything you have on a Peter Wilson. He is a porter here at Woodington and I want to know where he is, right now," she demanded. Looking back, she would accept that maybe her tone had been a little impolite. Maybe she could have softened the edges of her demands and made the whole experience one of smiles and good deeds. Instead, she managed to piss off the one person who could help them.

"If you'd like to take a seat, I'll need to speak with my superior," the spectacle-wearing woman answered, with about as much interest as a bored housewife watching paint dry in between doing the dishes and dusting. She returned to her computer, typing something quickly before hitting the send button a little harder than usual. Then she glared at the two detectives still yet to take a seat.

"I'm sorry." Sophie smiled, almost sincerely. "I'm not sure I made myself clear enough." She moved closer to the desk, the smile dropping from her face as her palms made contact and she leaned into the woman's space. "Get me everything you have on file on Peter Wilson, now!" She spoke the words clearly, each one its own little command as she glared, her eyes darkening as her facial features tightened.

"I...I've sent an email..."

"Not good enough. Get me the information or I will arrest you for interfering with a police investigation." This time she reached into her back pocket and pulled out a pair of handcuffs, dangled them in front of her, and asked again. "Peter Wilson."

Chapter Twenty-Five

Sophie Whitton stormed out of the hospital like a woman possessed. She had a cigarette in her hand already, and the minute she passed the exit doors, it was lit and she was sucking the toxic smoke down deep into her lungs.

"Fuck it!" she screamed. A woman with a small child instantly took a wide berth to avoid her. Others turned their heads and looked her way, old women shaking theirs in disgust at the foul tirade. She didn't care as she took another inhalation. The small white tube of poison felt good between her fingers.

"What now?" Branson asked. It was a valid question, but one she wasn't sure she had an answer to. Peter Wilson was not on shift today. He wasn't due in for another 24 hours, and all the files could tell them was that he had worked previously for a care home in town and at a baker's. His name hadn't flagged anything when they had checked him on the Criminal Records Bureau. The address they had on file was the same as the one the police were currently searching.

"I don't know...I..." She stopped mid-sentence and dropped the cigarette to the ground, crushing it with her boot. "I've got an idea...last time I was at the Duck, he was there."

Branson twisted his wrist around and checked his watch. The sun was well past the yardarm, as his old dad used to say. "So, what are we waiting for? Let's go." Sophie nodded and followed as he set off for the car.

"I hate these vests," she whined to herself as she fidgeted about and tried to adjust it. "I swear, if the fucker even tries to stab me, I'll murder him."

~Doll~

The Duck and Hound was exactly as she remembered it from her visit a few nights ago. It used to be a dark and dingy little place that had seen better days, then one of those modern breweries had taken over and pumped a shed load of cash into it, focusing on the fact that it was central to the police station, hospital, and fire brigade. It quickly became the go-to place for almost all of the emergency services to head to whenever they had some down time.

Behind the bar was the same guy from that night too. He didn't look quite so friendly when he first laid eyes on the pair of them. It was clear they were not here to enjoy a cold beverage, and he seemed a little out of sorts about that.

"Officers," he acknowledged, slowly drying a pint glass with a dishtowel. "Same as before?" he suggested to Whitton with a grin. She supposed he thought he was being clever. She held his stare and produced a photocopy of Peter Wilson's driving license.

"You seen him lately?" she asked, sliding the piece of paper across the bar. He moved his eyes downwards and glanced at the photograph.

"Wasn't he in here the other night too?" he answered, having scanned the image again.

Sophie couldn't actually remember that detail. "What's your name?" she asked him, changing the subject away from the night she was drunk.

"Tony," he answered. He didn't sound like a Tony. She would lay money he was an Anthony and had shortened it to fit in.

"Tony, have you seen him or not?" she repeated, her patience waning. He placed the glass down alongside the dishtowel and sniffed.

"Yeah, he left about thirty minutes ago with that blonde." Sophie felt the hairs on her neck rise at the mention of a possible new victim.

"What blonde?" Branson asked. Leaning on the bar, he studied the barman a little harder.

Tony looked back towards Whitton and added. "The one she left with the other night."

~Doll~

Whitton dragged Branson back out to the car, knocking over chairs and barging customers as they went. Pints of beer sloshed over her arm as she moved with lightning speed.

"We need to go, now!" she screamed at him as he fumbled in his pocket for the car keys. "Gimme the keys, I know where we're going."

She didn't care about the weather this time. Snow and ice were nothing but an inconvenience as she put her foot down, weaving and lurching through the traffic, clipping a kerb and just missing parked cars as they slid on the patches of black ice. The heater was on full blast, and yet she still felt chilled to the bone.

Time seemed to slow as her mind raced and tried to work out how long Rachel had been alone with him. How much damage could he do in that time? What the hell was she doing with him anyway?

Jeff had called it in. Backup in the form of uniformed officers was on its way, but he knew already that Whitton was going to get them there first, unless she killed them both instead.

Skidding to a halt, Sophie could see the lights on in Rachel's living room. It was quiet in the small street. Too cold for night time strolls or dog walking. She ran from the car, with Jeff hot on her heels, up the path to the doorway she had used so often lately. She had already made the decision to just kick the door in. There was no way she was going to give him any chance.

As they reached the door, Jeff tapped her shoulder. He didn't want to suggest that as a woman she wasn't capable, but for speed, his bulkier size was going to make this a lot simpler if it was him that shouldered the lock.

"Police!"

Chapter Twenty-Six

The call from Saint came ten minutes too late. He had captured Peter Wilson when he had returned to his home and was now taking him back to the station for questioning.

Rachel was standing in the kitchen. Jeff made a hasty retreat back out to the car, the chill of the night air preferable to the heated argument between the two women inside. Arms crossed against her chest, Rachel looked every bit as annoyed as she had sounded.

"Look, I came here to save you...not pick a fight." Sophie attempted to cool things down. Rachel had been somewhat angered by the presence of two police officers barging into her living room. The splintered front door hanging off its hinges, allowing the cold air in, did nothing to cool her temper.

"Save me?" she huffed as she threw up her hands. "From what? Who? Pete? I told you, he just gave me a lift home and then he left."

"I can't go into detail, okay? You have to just trust me on this," she implored, edging across the room slowly. "We need to speak to him, urgently, and when the guy at the bar said you'd left with him...I just..." By now she was standing in front of Rachel, who still had her arms wrapped around herself as she listened to Sophie, listened to what she wasn't telling her.

"You think he is..."

"I can't...he is a person of interest, okay? And I..." Sophie reached out and tucked an errant piece of hair back behind the blonde's ear. "I was concerned that he..."

"Go, you need to go and do your job." Her voice was quiet, understanding, her manner now calmer. Whitton smiled and turned to leave. "Detective?"

"Yeah?" Sophie stopped and twisted back around to face her.

"I want my door fixed." She smirked. "And I expect you here, later. I'll need warming up after this."

Sophie nodded, her dark hair flopping forward as she continued to stare. "I'll do my best."

~Doll~

Peter Wilson sat alone in Interview Room Two. His fingertip was scratching lightly against the desk in a nervous manner, adding to the already numerous markings etched into the wood from previous occupants. The room was small, and the walls felt as though they were closing in; that was the point. No window, no natural light. They had left him there for the last thirty minutes while they gathered their thoughts and paperwork, and let him stew.

Although they did have a warrant for his arrest, Dale had used his initiative. When Wilson had arrived home to find police officers swarming his flat, he hadn't made a run for it or attempted to evade them. In fact, he appeared confused more than anything.

So, Dale had simply 'invited' him to attend the station and talk to them, and he had accepted.

The door opened, and Whitton strode in with purpose, Saint following. Neither spoke as they both took a seat opposite the young man who was now chewing on his nail. Whitton kept her eyes firmly on him as Dale unwrapped a tape and placed it into the cassette player.

Wilson blushed under the attention, fidgeting in his seat and looking away. He looked guilty, but now that Whitton had eyes on him, she wasn't quite so sure what of.

Dale spoke clearly for the tape. "This interview is being undertaken by myself, Detective Sergeant Dale Saint, in Interview Room Two, Woodington Police Station." He added the date and time, all the while looking straight at Peter Wilson. "I am interviewing...Please say your name for the record."

"Uh, Peter, Peter Wilson."

"Also present is Detective Inspector Sophie Whitton. For the record, Mr Wilson has not requested a solicitor at this present time. However, he is aware that he may stop this interview at any time and request a solicitor to consult."

Whitton opened a file and slid out a piece of A4 paper. His eyes lowered to the table, and Peter Wilson watched intently as she pushed the paper across the desk and turned it so that it was the correct way up for him to read. His rights in writing.

"I must repeat the caution for you. You do not have to say anything. But, it may harm your defence if you do not mention when questioned something which you later rely on in court. Anything you do say may be given in evidence." She said the words without emotion, never once taking her eyes from him. "Do you understand this caution?"

He nodded. A bead of sweat began to trickle slowly down his pale forehead and he gulped visibly.

"Please speak clearly for the tape," Dale interjected, and Wilson looked up at him and nodded once more.

"Yes, I understand."

"Would you like a drink?" Sophie asked. He looked like he was about to faint. He nodded once more before remembering the tape.

"Yes, please." Nobody moved, and he wondered if they were just playing with him. Both officers continued to sit there observing him. He swallowed, his throat dry and coarse. He licked his lips and tried to calm his breathing. There was a knock, and a uniformed officer entered with a plastic cup of water. He placed it down on the table and retreated without a word.

"Do you know why you're here, Peter?" Sophie asked gently. She wasn't looking at him now. Instead she was pretending to read something important in the file. When he didn't reply, she looked up and smiled. "No?"

"N-no." He shook his head. Silence from both detectives once again left him fidgeting.

"Do you watch the news, Peter? Read any papers?" she continued.

"Not really, no."

She smiled once more at him and settled back in her chair, steepling her fingers together as she considered how to continue.

"Recently, Peter, we discovered a body." She watched his reaction. His pupils grew darker, and the beads of sweat had now multiplied. "Would you know anything about that, Pete?"

Swallowing hard, his voice stuck in his throat as he tried to answer. Dale pushed the glass of water towards him and they watched as he drained the cup. "I...no, I...What body?"

She ignored the question and took her time before following up. "You see, the problem is, Pete, that we think maybe you know quite a lot about it."

"No...I mean, why would I?"

"You tell me." She sat forward and placed her hands down flat on the desk, her dark eyes fixed with his before she looked down at her file once more. "You were born on the 15th October in 1988, right?"

"Right, uh no...'87."

"'87?"

"No, 1988." He nodded. Dale leant into her and pretended to whisper something important. She nodded and played along before turning her attention back to Wilson.

"Do you have a brother?"

"No."

"Do you know a Gloria Armstrong?" Once again she watched for his reaction. His cheeks had paled and his gaze had dropped to his lap. He shook his head violently. "For the tape, please."

"No." His voice now was barely a whisper.

"Is that a no?" Dale prodded further.

This time he nodded. "Yes, I mean no, no I don't know her."

"Have you ever lived or visited an address in Myrtle Street?"

"No."

"Is your name really Peter Wilson?"

"Yes." The beads of sweat were now more like a fountain. He looked everywhere but at the two detectives.

"What's your mother's name?"

"What?" The question threw him and he looked from one to the other, puzzlement creating a frown.

"Your mother's name Peter, what is it?" She kept that friendly smile on her face, though she would admit it probably looked like a smug 'I already know the answer' grin to him.

"Look, I don't understand where...Why am I here? What does my mother have to do with anything?"

"Answer the question please, Peter."

He picked at the quick around his finger. His breathing more rapid now as he tried to work out what they wanted with him. "Do I need a lawyer?"

"Do you think you need one? Is there something you need to tell us?" Sophie continued to keep her voice neutral and calm. She had him on the rack, she knew that. But she still wasn't quite so sure it was for the Doll Maker crimes.

"I don't know. I don't know why I am here or what it is you think I've done." He was getting wound up now, fretting and clearly hiding something. He was evasive and changing the subject, and he was just where she wanted him to be.

Chapter Twenty-Seven

It was nearing midnight. Peter Wilson had been in the interview room for more than an hour as Whitton and Saint continued to ask the same questions over and over.

"Did you know a William Wilson?" Sophie asked. His Adam's apple bobbed up and down visibly and she caught herself smiling, this time because she knew she had him. "Gregory?"

He fought the urge to cry, but his eyes were wet with tears. One by one they trickled down his cheek. His eyes closed, and he dropped his head to his chest and sobbed.

"I can't, I'm sorry...I'm so sorry." His voice cracked and his shoulders visibly shook. "I didn't mean to..."

"Gregory?" She called his name gently, repeating it until he finally looked up at her. "Gregory, we're going to take a short break now. Do you understand?" He nodded, and this time she let it go. "For the record, Mr Wilson, aka Gregory Armstrong, has nodded his assent."

~Doll~

Closing the door behind them, she instructed the uniformed officer from before to take him in something to eat and drink.

"What the hell are we stopping for?" Dale said as they walked towards the exit door.

"Because, he was drinking earlier, and he is going to talk. Whatever he is hiding, whatever crime he is involved in, he wants to talk about it," she replied, pulling a cigarette from the pack. She offered one to Dale, but he shook his head no.

"So, let him!" Dale insisted.

"We will, I just wanna give him five minutes. Let him stew," she said, lighting up and inhaling. She checked her phone and wondered if Rachel was waiting up. Flicking open the message app, she sent a quick message, not expecting a reply. "I don't want a fancy lawyer saying we coerced a drunken man into admitting anything."

Rachel: *There is a spare key in the key safe. The code is 3024.*

She smiled to herself and wondered why it was she had never felt the need to keep Yvonne up to date with how long she would be working till. Maybe she just wasn't wearing rose-tinted glasses anymore over her relationship with Yvonne.

With her cigarette finished, she slapped Dale on the back. "Right, let's get this over with."

~Doll~

Standing outside of the door, Sophie held off from opening it. Instead she took a moment, got her head into the right space. Previously she had played nice cop, lulling him into a sense of easiness with her. She'd been understanding, smiling and polite with him so far, and he felt comfortable with her. But now she was going to change that up. Now she was going to rip him apart until she got the truth from him.

Turning the doorknob, she pushed the door open hard and let it bang against the wall. She noticed him jump out of his skin and place a hand across his chest.

"Sorry, did I scare you?" she asked without even looking at him. She pulled the chair out, letting it scrape against the floor, the kind of noise that made your teeth hurt.

Dale hit record on the tape and ran through the details they needed to have recorded for evidence. When he was done, he turned to Whitton and waited for her to continue.

"So, Gregory. Let's start with why you killed your mother." She looked at him now and witnessed the shock on his face.

"What? I didn't...I haven't even seen her since before Easter."

"I'm going to warn you just once Gregory, lying isn't going to help you now." She pulled out a photograph of the skeletal remains of Gloria Armstrong sitting tied to the chair and pushed it towards him.

He flew back in his chair as though touched by something evil. "I didn't... I didn't do that, I wouldn't. Look, she was alive and up to her old tricks when I saw her."

"The thing is, Gregory, we can't really believe a word you say, can we? I mean, you've lied about who you are for years, and when I asked if you knew Gloria, you categorically said you didn't...so?"

"But..."

"No buts, Greg," Dale interjected. "This is serious, and right now you're looking good for it."

"Good for what...what are you talking about? I haven't seen her in months. I hated her..." He stopped talking abruptly, aware of what he had just said.

"You hated her? Do you think whoever did this was particularly fond of her?" Dale continued, tapping his finger continuously against the photograph of Gloria Armstrong. "I'm willing to bet that the person that did this hated her too, don't ya think so?"

"I don't know! It wasn't me."

The room smelt musty. He was sweating, and the walls were definitely closing in on him. "Why did you change your name?" Sophie asked, trying to confuse him with questions, keep him answering until eventually he tripped up.

"I just did."

"Why that name? Did you know William?"

"Yes." Sophie gave herself a mental high five. "Yes, I knew him," he finally relented.

"Did you murder your mother?" Dale continued.

"NO!" He stood up abruptly and the chair fell backwards. "I didn't kill her."

"Sit down please," Sophie asked as he paced the small space on that side of the desk. "Gregory, sit down, *now!*" Her raised voice seemed to resonate with him and he stopped in his tracks, picked up the chair and sat down, like a good little boy. "How did you know William Wilson?"

"I met him in care. We were in the same home for a while." He held his head in his hands and rocked back and forth.

"Did you kill him too?" Dale asked. Gregory looked up at him and shook his head.

"You don't get it, you'll never get it...*I didn't kill anyone.*" He spelt out the last four words hoping they would understand.

"How long did the abuse go on for?" Sophie asked. Subject change again; keep him on his toes. His head swiveled so fast she thought he might get whiplash. "Your mother? She used you as a special...gift? For the men that paid, right?"

"How do you know that?" he asked. His face flushed, and she thought he might actually throw up. There was a metal bin to her right. Lifting it, she placed it on the desk with a bang in front of him.

"Don't miss," she warned him, but he ignored her and placed the bin back down on the blue linoleum flooring, still within easy reach.

"That woman...my mother, she is...was, evil." He spoke quietly, a single tear sliding down his left cheek. "I don't have any other word for her, she was just evil." His eyes closed as he composed himself. "I was six when she first introduced me to one."

"One?" Dale asked, pen at the ready. Gregory Armstrong sneered at him.

"Of her punters. I was six, she called me from my room and led me to hers...I had no idea who he was, she called him Uncle Terry and then she left me with him." He picked again at the skin around his fingernails.

Whitton didn't need the details. They had seen the photos and had a clear idea about the likes of 'Uncle Terry,' so she moved him on. He looked at her, grateful. He had spent years trying to forget all of this.

"What age were you when you went into care?"

"On and off from eight. It all depended on what she was caught doing. Few weeks if it was shoplifting, might be a few months for drug offenses." He gazed off into the distance. "Happiest days of my life were spent at St Mildred's."

"And that's where you met William?" Sophie nudged a little further.

"Yeah. He was 14, I was a year older. I might have been happier at 'dred's, but that didn't mean it was easy there. Will, he looked out for me."

"And you repaid him by killing him and taking his identity?" Dale accused. He glared across the table at the bleached-haired man who seemed to grow smaller with every passing minute.

"No...I'd never, Will was like a brother...he was all I had, and she couldn't wait to take that from me too!" he bellowed. Sophie sat back in her chair and waited him out, waited for the anger to subside. She was getting hot; the room was stuffy, and she really wanted a cigarette. Actually, she really wanted to be in bed, wrapped around Rachel.

"What do you mean by that? What did she do to Will?" Whitton asked the question as she pulled off her jumper. The shirt beneath was a little creased, but that was far from being top of her list of concerns.

"The last time I was sent home...Will turned up, he said he had run away and...I sneaked him in. She was off her face most of the time, barely even noticed me unless a punter was around. Of course, just my luck one of her weirdos wanted to pay for me and so she came looking, found Will in my room." He licked his lips and coughed. Sophie reached out to a small cupboard and pulled a bottle of water from it and passed it to him. He took a long swig. "Thanks. I did as she wanted, but afterwards she wanted to know who Will was and why he was there. Then she did something I never thought she would...she said he could stay."

Both detectives were listening intently. Most of the time people sat across from them like this and tried to bullshit their way through it. It didn't feel like that this time. Gregory was unloading.

"So, Will moved in properly and social services were okay with that?"

He shook his head. "No, I don't think they knew. Will was always running away... he lived with a nice couple once, but they wanted to be his parents and he just didn't want that. He was 14; for him it was too late for that, and they couldn't cope with his getting up to no good. They were good people, churchgoers, and he was a dope smoking, shoplifting Goth." He chuckled at the memory of his friend. "He was almost old enough to leave anyway. I guess they just forgot about him, but we never heard from social services."

"Why is Will buried in the garden of your mother's home?"

"Like everything she touched, she changed him. Showed him the money he could earn if he just...She used him, like she used me, only I never earned anything from it," he said bitterly. "I used to go out when they had punters around, she didn't seem to care now that she had Will willingly going with them, and it meant..." He looked away guiltily. "It meant that they left me alone."

"So, she was pimping him out?"

"Yeah, I came home one night and she was screaming at me the minute I walked through the door. I couldn't understand anything she was saying, I'd never seen her like that before. She dragged me up the stairs and...Will, he was...he was naked and laying on the bed." His face scrunched up, the tears freely flowing. "He had...his ankles were tied to the bed and he had a huge gash across the back of his head. There was a lot of blood, the sheets were covered, and she was still crying and screeching."

Now they were getting somewhere. She glanced at the clock on the wall and noted that it was almost 1 a.m. At some point she was going to call this a night, but right now she was going to let him sing.

"I didn't know, but the pair of them had taken on some different clients. Ones that liked to ya know, get rough. Inflicting pain, that kind of thing. This one that night had paid extra to hit Will. He had agreed, the lure of the money see? It went too far, this guy had brought with him a bat, like a kid's cricket bat thing and...we buried him. She said no-one would believe us, I'd go to prison if anyone found out, she would tell everyone that I did it."

Chapter Twenty-Eight

Creeping into Rachel's house at 2 a.m., she needed to be a ninja. The woman had stuff. Shoes littered the little space by the door, all out of order and tossed aside as weary feet finally shooed them away. At least the door looked as good as new.

Her coat was thrown haphazardly over the bannister along with her bag, the strap holding the coat in its place. Everything was so different from the life that Sophie had been leading before. Yvonne was a stickler for "a place for everything and everything in its place," and that suited Sophie. She liked order, and yet chaos seemed to follow her anyway. In reality, Rachel was organised chaos. Her job entailed spending every second of the day micro managing germs and cleanliness. When she got home, the last thing she wanted to do was tidy up. She was often exhausted, and so clothes fell to the floor and stayed there till washing day. The dust accumulated until Maggie popped in for the two hours Rachel paid 'Housemaids' to have her stuff given the once over. She was pretty good at washing up. With just herself to feed each night, there usually wasn't much to do, and it was easy enough to keep on top of.

Her uniforms went to the cleaners once a week, and everything else got shoved into the machine on her day off. The only time she had to panic was if she had taken on overtime, and then it was a quick trip to the supermarket for some cheap new undies and socks. Of course, she now had an entire drawer for each.

The stairs creaked as Sophie tiptoed upwards. One by one she winced at what seemed like the loudest noise on Earth. For all its quaintness, this old cottage had a lot of things about it that Sophie would gladly be rid of.

She crept inside the bedroom, the only light coming from the moon against the thin curtains. Stripping down to her underwear, she folded her clothes neatly and placed them in a pile on small bucket chair that Rachel had probably acquired as somewhere to sit and read, but had quickly become another place to throw her discarded clothes.

The bed was warm. There was evidence of an electric blanket beneath the sheets. Inching her now-naked body closer to Rachel, she held her breath so as not to wake her. Closer and closer she pressed herself against the warm body, her right arm snaking around her waist, clutching her hand against the soft stomach beneath the button-up pajama top. She stroked her thumb across the fading scar that she knew was there. Rachel mumbled and groaned in her sleep as she pressed herself back against Sophie, her own hand moving to cover her lover's.

"Is it him?" she asked, her words slurred with sleep.

"No, I don't think so. Go to sleep."

"I am asleep, stop talking to me."

Sophie smiled as the gentle snoring immediately resumed. As she lay there in the dark, her mind went back to the moment when the interview with Gregory Armstrong had come to its conclusion.

She was pretty much convinced that he wasn't the Doll Maker. Of course, they were keeping him in lockup anyway. The CPS would have to decide what to do with him with regard to William Wilson's death and subsequent burial. Barnard would be able to tell them definitively if Gregory had had anything to do with murdering three women and his mother. DNA tests against the hair they had found on the body of Sandra Bancroft would prove or disprove absolutely. She just had to wait.

But the one thing she was sure of was that this wasn't over.

~Doll~

A mechanical clanging and banging woke her. The refuse collection was taking place. The huge bulky machine lifted each and every wheelie bin along the street, emptied it and dumped it back on the ground, where it was noisily wheeled back to its home and delivered with a further bang.

Her eyes were gritty, and it was still somewhat dark outside as they fluttered open and shut. There was a warmth beside her that signaled Rachel had no intentions of getting up. Her softer body fit snuggly alongside Sophie's bonier one.

Quite often she would wonder what it was about herself that attracted these beautiful women into her life. Rachel was voluptuous in all the right areas; she wasn't skinny like Sophie. She was womanly, rounded and sexy. She had boobs, where Sophie lacked. Her backside was something to grab, unlike Sophie whose trousers would fall down without a belt.

"You're thinking too hard over there," a mumbled voice said sleepily.

"How do you do that?" Sophie smiled.

"I felt you stir, then tense up, so you're obviously thinking too hard." Rachel turned and tucked herself even closer against her. "Wanna share?"

"No."

"Oh come on, tell me what gets you so tense at..." She checked the clock on the bedside cupboard. "6:36 in the morning?" Her fingers instantly worked to relieve the tension.

"Fuck." Sophie shuddered at the touch. "How are you so good at that too?"

"At what?" Her lips were nipping now at the skin available, gentle kisses along a collarbone and shoulder.

"You know exactly what." Sophie gasped, the tension easing off before another kind of tension took its place. She grabbed the hem of Rachel's sleep top and lifted, the small scar now visible. "How did you get this?" she asked, sliding her finger gently over it.

"Oh, no, no, no, you are not changing the conversation, Detective." Rachel smiled as she rolled herself up and over the supine cop. Sophie considered the question again, then using her strength and with the element of surprise on her side, she swiftly reversed their positions.

"I was wondering why I seem to attract such beautiful women." She studied her, watched as her head tilted and her eyes softened.

"You think I'm beautiful?"

"Amazingly beautiful." Sophie leant down and kissed her, felt the reciprocation until a firm palm pressed against her chest.

"I'm not perfect." She indicated the scar. "An accident when I was a kid." She brushed it off as unimportant. "And I need to lose a few pounds." She blushed and looked away.

"No, you don't need to do that. You're perfect just the way you are," Sophie replied and waited until Rachel finally returned her gaze. They stayed that way, eyes locked together as Rachel considered her words.

"You're kinda hot in a 'doesn't give a shit' kinda way. And the way you care about the people around you, people you don't even know...I like that. You're intense and brusque and yet, deep inside here." She pressed her palm against Sophie's heart. "There's a passion that burns so hard I can almost feel it on my fingertips when I touch you."

Sophie placed her fingers around the wrist of the palm that still rested on her chest and moved it away, pinning it to the bed by the side of Rachel's head. This time when she kissed her, it was harder. Their lips pressed together forcefully, bodies joining together in an urgent, slick need.

"And you smell good," Rachel laughed. "So good."

Chapter Twenty-Nine

Being locked away was not a feeling he enjoyed. It was something he had endured before at school and he would get through it again, but he didn't enjoy it.

He couldn't help but laugh at the irony of it all. He had spent a lifetime trying to be someone else. His father had never really been a dad. Even now, the old man was nothing more than a drunk. His mother though, she had loved him, but she had always put the old man first. He was so angry at her for that. Always too busy living the life of a whore, demeaning herself all for his father's pleasure.

And now, here they all were, wanting him. They could wait though; he would just sit this out. Eventually they would realise they had the wrong man, and he would need to be extra careful if he was to finish what he started.

It was simple really, though none of them understood it or had a clue why he was doing what he had to do. The bitch had gone and died, that was why he had to do this. It was her fault.

He recalled watching his mother, in the car that night when Tiffany was still with them. All four of them were driving home from another party that he didn't want to go to. Tiffany was upset. His mother had said nothing, pushed them into the car and climbed into the passenger seat beside their father. He was drunk again, but she still let him drive. He was tired and had fallen asleep next to Tiffany. There was a huge bang, the car tipped and turned, they were rolling. Everything went dark and when he woke, his mother was in the driver's seat.

He wanted to tell the police, but she stopped him. "Nobody would understand," she told him. "It's better this way." Better for whom?

They had all gotten lucky that night. How many times had they had to suffer because his mother would let his father enjoy himself too much?

~Doll~

Woken by the sounds of small children squealing in excitement, Dale Saint had no hesitation in smiling, even though he hadn't gotten in until 2 a.m. and was barely able to open his eyes. He could hear Becky telling Ella and Harry to calm down. Up until a week ago, Harriet had ignored anybody calling her Harry, but now since beginning play school, Harry was the only name she would answer to. He liked it; it suited the little tomboy.

"Daddy!" Ella shouted, grinning her toothy smile as she ran and launched herself onto the bed. She landed with a knee that almost connected with his vital parts.

"Hey, Ella Bella," he groaned, catching her in his arms before she could do any major damage.

"Daddy, Mummy said you was sleeping."

"I was trying to, but then I heard my little angels having all that fun." He tickled her, and she giggled and kicked.

"Stop, Daddy, I'm gonna wet myself." She laughed some more, her dark blonde hair flopping all over her face as she wriggled in his arms.

"Sorry, I did try and keep them quiet." Becky smiled from the doorway as Harry came bustling between her mother's legs to join her sister. "Do you need to get up or...I can take them out for a walk around the park if you want to get a few more hours in?"

"Nah, it's okay...we got a break in the case so, I'll go back in as soon as I'm up. Breakfast first?"

"You got him?" Becky asked as she moved to sit herself on the edge of the bed, pulling her dressing gown a little tighter. The girls were playing now with Dale's phone, a game of Angry Birds.

"No, well Sophie doesn't think it's him. I guess we will find out soon enough once Barnard runs his tests."

"And how is Sophie?"

"She seems okay. She and Yvonne, they split up."

Becky nodded. "I guessed as much. I overheard some of the staff discussing Rachel's new girlfriend." She used to her fingers to indicate speech marks. "The butch cop."

"Seriously?" Dale asked. "She hasn't said anything."

"Apparently a few of the girls saw them at the pub the other night. They left together," she whispered,

"Wow, you saying she's been having an affair?" He shook his head. The girls were jumping up and down on the bed now, giggling and trying to bounce higher.

Becky shrugged. "I dunno, I warned Rachel off weeks ago." She blushed a little. "God, it was getting embarrassing, the way she fawned over Sophie anytime she saw her." She giggled at the memory. "Like a bitch on heat, I tell ya." They both fell about laughing.

"What's a bitch?" Harry asked.

~Doll~

DNA samples had been sent to Barnard first thing that morning. When Whitton arrived at the station, her first port of call was to the cells to check on Gregory Armstrong, AKA Peter Wilson.

The small holding area downstairs was quiet when she arrived. The desk sergeant sat hunched over his desk reading the early morning copy of the *Herald*. One hand held the paper in place, ready to turn the next page, whilst the other held a half-eaten bacon sarnie. Droplets of brown sauce dripped onto the page below.

"Morning Sergeant Davis, how is Mr Armstrong this morning?" she asked politely enough. Being tired wasn't his fault, so she held off the crankiness as best she could. It was colder down here; the draft from the doors opening and closing keeping the air cool and unwelcoming.

"Well, he seemed fine enough half hour ago when I took him his morning tea and toast. To be fair, he hasn't given us any hassle. Slept most the night and when he was awake, he just sat there quietly."

"Good, I doubt he will be here much longer."

He nodded and went back to reading the cricket story that had captivated him earlier. She wandered along the short corridor and found the cell marked with Gregory's name, flipped the metal flap that would allow her to look inside, and saw him just sitting there as Davis had said. He glanced up briefly before his eyes dropped back to the floor. She clipped the flap shut again and turned on her heels, glancing at the CCTV as she passed. He hadn't moved.

~Doll~

"Why does he make the doll?" Dale asked as he leant back in his chair and let it wheel away from the desk a little. He raised his feet and placed them on the desk, looking around at the team. Blank faces stared back. "I mean, if we can work that out, then maybe we can get him to talk, make him break."

Whitton sighed and stood abruptly. "It's not him," she said. Grabbing her mug, she crossed the room and poured a fresh coffee.

"How can you just dismiss him so easily?"

"Because, it's not him!" she repeated, stirring the sugar in and taking a sip. She winced as the heated liquid burnt her upper lip.

"Everything points to him...it's his mother." He placed one index finger against the other and counted off one. "It's his home...he knew Wilson...he took Wilson's identity, for fuck's sake." He had counted off the four reasons, but kept his gaze firmly on her.

"Where does the male victim fit?"

He shrugged. "I dunno."

"Exactly, because he doesn't, not with Gregory. Think about it, if Gregory Armstrong was the killer, he wouldn't be sending us a message with creepy dolls. He would be attacking only women that reminded him of his mother, or men that reminded him of his abusers."

"Yeah, okay I get that."

"Right, so look at the victims of the Doll Maker. Middle aged woman he tortures. Then there are three younger women that he is almost reverent with, dressing them in fine clothing, fuck he even cried over one." She almost snorted at the irony of it all. "And then there is the attack on Price, an older male. What does that say to you, Dale?"

Once more he shrugged. "I dunno, that he is a looney?"

She nodded and laughed. "Yeah, he is definitely not all there, but it says one thing to me...family. Mother, sisters, father."

"Okay, but I still think Gregory Armstrong is a solid candidate."

"I'm going for a smoke." Ignoring him was going to be the best policy. He was right, everything pointed to Armstrong, but she would place her career on it that when the results came back from Barnard, it wouldn't be him.

It was still snowing outside. This was turning out to be the worst winter they had seen in years, maybe even decades. It was at least two foot deep in areas that hadn't been trampled on, though mostly it was mush and ice where footsteps had trodden it down and the salt had melted it. Someone had built a snowman in the corner of the yard, two old truncheons for arms and a fag butt smile. She heard the door open and close and waited to see which one of them it would be that had joined her.

"Got a spare?" Dale asked, moving side to side from one foot to the other to keep warm.

"I thought you'd given up." She handed the pack to him. He pulled one out and closed the lid, handing them back to her while she flicked the lighter. Cupping the small blue flame with both hands, he lit the cigarette and took a drag.

"I have, especially if Becky asks." He grinned.

"Don't worry, I won't grass you up." They stood conspiratorially in the doorway together: jackets done up, hats on and scarves wrapped around necks, bracing themselves against the cold. It was definitely going to be a white Christmas.

"When do you think we will hear from Barnard?" Dale asked.

"Dunno, he put a rush on it but, you know what these things are like. We're still waiting to find out if the hair matched Gloria."

"Yeah, well I still think he did it." Sophie rolled her eyes and sighed audibly. "Why are you so adamant that he didn't? I don't get it...everything points to him."

"I just know...call it gut instinct."

"Or you're thinking with ya..."

"My what?" She glared at him. He looked contrite as he looked to the ground and took a drag. His cheeks flushed. "Go on, what am I thinking with instead of my brain?"

"Come on Soph, all this shit with Yvonne...and now Rachel..."

"What?" She threw what was left of the cigarette down on the ground and stepped up into his space. "What did you just say? Rachel?"

"Look, I didn't mean anything by it...it's just, you gotta admit you've been off the pace a bit lately."

"Off the pace? What the fuck, Dale?" The cold didn't touch her now as the heat of rage pulsed through her. "Listen, my relationships are exactly that, mine! What I do outside of work has no effect on my judgement or ability to do the job."

He held his hands up, fag held tightly between his lips. "Alright, alright...I'm just saying we shouldn't write him off, that's all."

"No, we should, but hey I'm too busy fucking everything up to make that call right!" She barged past him and pushed the door open, letting it bang loudly behind her.

Chapter Thirty

With Barnard's confirmation that the hair found on Sandra Bancroft didn't belong to Gregory Armstrong and was no relation to Gloria Armstrong either, he was released on bail the following day. The CPS were still deciding whether he would face charges for the disposal of a corpse, failing to report a death, or worse still, a murder, but that wasn't Whitton's concern any longer.

Sheepishly, Dale arrived with three cups of coffee in a cardboard tray in one hand and a paper bag containing a single salted caramel muffin in the other. Jeff made a grab for one of the coffees, mumbling a quick thanks before he sipped at it and winced. The Christmas-themed cardboard takeaway insulation cup had done its job thoroughly. Whitton looked up as Dale slid the bag across the desk to her and placed a cup down next to it.

"What's this?" she said, pulling the bag closer. She knew it had to be a cake; it was from the coffee shop.

"An apology." He grimaced a little. "You were right," he added as she opened the bag and took a peek inside. Her favourite.

"I was right?" she inquired with a tilt of her head.

"Yeah, it ain't my place to butt in on your love life."

She grinned at him. "Don't forget it." She pulled the bag open and reached in. Sticky chocolate and caramel attached to her fingertips instantly. Branson laughed and shook his head.

"He stuck his nose in?" Jeff asked, still laughing. "You're lucky you ain't sporting a black eye, mate." Whitton smirked at him, while Dale attempted to laugh that idea off, knowing full well that he was right too. "Anyway," Jeff continued now that he had both of their attention. "I was thinking about something that didn't make much sense."

"Go on," Sophie encouraged, sitting back in her chair as she cradled the hot drink in both hands.

"Well, why did he get rid of the car?"

"What do you mean?" She sat up now, intrigued with the question. He scratched his scalp and perched himself on the corner of her desk.

"So, you have a car, right? A cheap little run around that's popular and nobody is really onto you, why burn the car? What spooked him into getting rid of it now?" Whitton and Saint both nodded, listening to the point he was making. "We never made it known to the papers. The only time we've mentioned it is house-to-house calls."

"So, you think maybe we've spoken to him?" Dale asked.

Jeff shrugged. "I dunno, it was just a thought, that's all."

"It's a good point, Jeff. He could very easily be someone we've talked to. Let's get some residential information together, get all the notes."

~Doll~

Fifteen households had been canvassed following Sandra Bancroft's body being discovered. Twelve were ruled out instantly. Eight single mothers, an 86-year-old single widower, and three couples well into their seventies. That left three potential people of interest.

"Jeff, this is your baby," Sophie told him. "Run background checks on all three households. I want to know everything there is to know about all three men and the two older teenagers. Anything that sticks out, no matter how small."

"Sure boss, can I get Andy on it with me? Will be quicker if there are two of us," he said, smiling at her. He was charming as well as good-looking, and Whitton had the idea that when he used that smile on other women, it weakened their knees.

"Yeah Jeff, go for it." She turned her attention to Saint. "I want a list of every officer, S.O.C.O...anyone that's involved in this case that would know about the car."

"What are you suggesting?" Dale asked quietly. He took her by the elbow and turned them away from potential listening ears. "You think it's someone on the force?"

"I think a lot of things, Dale. I'm not prepared to ignore the fact that it *could* be. I don't *think* it is, but I want it ruled out," she confirmed, her jaw tight with tension. "And keep it on the lowdown, okay? I don't want anyone on this team feeling like I don't trust them."

"Sure thing." He placed a calming palm around her bicep. "I'll snoop about a bit, see if there is anything that stands out."

"Good." She checked her watch. It was gone 9 p.m. "Okay, listen up!" she called out to the team. "One more hour digging and then I want everyone down at the Duck. We all need a few hours away from this. Let your hair down for an hour and relax, come at this with fresh eyes in the morning. That means no getting pissed, alright?"

~Doll~

Watching them all run around like headless chickens was almost funny and yet, it pissed him off. They still had no idea. Looking in all the wrong places, it would be a lifetime before there was any justice. She might be dead and he might be locked in his own alcohol-fueled prison, but that didn't mean the world shouldn't know what they were.

All those years he had spent trying to make her listen, desperately pleading with her to open her eyes and speak out. She didn't, and now, now the world needed to know that. The world needed to understand.

He was getting antsy trying to find the missing piece, but he was looking still. He would find him and when he did, it would almost be all over.

~Doll~

The pub was packed. Half the hospital staff seemed to be congregated around the bar holding some kind of celebratory drinking game that involved necking shots of something brightly coloured before slamming the glasses down on the counter and downing pints of lager. Christmas party season had arrived weeks ago and was showing no signs of ending until Christmas itself did. The sound of Bing Crosby warbling about how it was beginning to look a lot like Christmas blared out. Groups of nurses sang along, swaying from side to side as a guy in a suit wandered between them all holding up a bunch of mistletoe, snatching kisses from those drunk enough to fall for it.

Sophie found her team huddled around a tall table. Andy Bowen, Jeff Branson, and Dale Saint perched their backsides on bar stools while the rest of them just used the table to lean on or place empty glasses. Those were piling up, pint glasses stacked five high. Empty packets of peanuts and crisps littered the floor, along with the sticky puddles of spilt drinks.

"Hey boss, ya finally made it. We got ya a pint, but Andy drank it!" They all burst into laughter and raised their glasses. Whitton laughed at their cheek and turned towards the bar. It would take a lot of hard work to get through the crowd and find a member of staff to pull a pint, but tonight wasn't the night to be deterred.

It was at least four deep at the bar as she edged her way between backs and shoulders, dodging elbows that raised to sink another drink. When she managed to get two deep, she caught the eye of the barman.

"Tony, Tony! Pint of whatever's easiest," she called out. The bald head nodded at her as he reached for a clean glass.

"Hey you." A sultry voice appeared in her ear. "I am a little drunk and extremely horny."

Whitton turned to find Rachel leaning in towards her. "Oh yeah?" She felt the blonde's hands slide under her jacket, smoothing their way across her abdomen and inching lower towards the waistband of her trousers. The intense feeling of arousal shot through Sophie like an arrow hitting its target.

"Yeah." Green eyes burned into her own darker ones.

"Well, I am here with my entire team." Tony held the pint out for her and she took it, passing him a crisp new five pound note. "So, you're going to have to hold that thought for a bit longer."

"Okay, get me before you leave." And with that she was gone, lost in a crowd of drunks. Whitton chuckled to herself before heading back over to her team.

She could see them all laughing and kidding around. It was good to watch; working in this job didn't always allow for such frivolity. What they all saw on a daily basis would be enough to send most people fleeing, and yet, every day they got up and came back for more. She swallowed down half the pint in one swig.

"I'm telling ya though, this fucker, leaving the creepy little dolls? It's just not fucking normal, is it?" Ansu Patel said loudly to the group. Bouncing heads nodding the affirmative at his words. "I mean come on, who does that? And what is it with the three wise monkey shit?"

"Boss?" Jeff got her attention. She glanced at him, listening, but her eyes stayed firmly on Ansu and the others. "I checked out the households, there's nothing. Everyone has an alibi for at least one of the murders. There is no way any of them are responsible."

"Okay, cheers," she answered with a tight smile as she took a step forward towards the conversation. She listened intently as she sipped at her pint. It wasn't the kind of drink she would normally have, but it would suffice.

"And the car? Fucking burnt out just like that," Colleen O'Leary added with a click of her fingers before she downed the rest of her wine. Whitton followed suit and finished off her own drink too.

"Right, come on you lot, that's enough for tonight, eh? I want to see everyone bright and early in the morning. And I mean *everyone* in the office by seven," Whitton said. A chorus of groans and moans floated her way.

"Everything okay?" Dale asked as everyone else drank up and grabbed coats.

"Yeah, I think I know how he knows what we know," she said, expecting him to understand what she was talking about. The cocked eyebrow told her that he did. "I want you in early, Dale."

"I'll be there."

Chapter Thirty-One

"Don't tease me, Detective." Her voice was low and sultry. With only one drink in her system, Sophie had driven. Climbing inside the car, the already inebriated nurse had made a claim for her mouth. Sophie had succumbed instantly and allowed the intrusion of the enthusiastic tongue. Making out in the car like horny teenagers was exciting, but Sophie would rather not have an audience for the things she had planned tonight.

Rachel had grabbed her hand from where it rested on the gear stick and placed it high up her leg, pushing her dress out of the way and spreading her thighs just wide enough to enjoy the feeling of Sophie's fingers sliding between them, nudging at the apex of her arousal.

"Patience, Rachel." Sophie was concentrating on too many things. The weather was cold; it had snowed again earlier and iced over as the night wore on. The roads were treacherous. Her mind was also wandering to the idea that was forming in her head: Loose lips from her own team. And then there was Rachel whose shallow breaths and whimpers were turning her on as she drove. Her fingers teasing swollen, slick folds did nothing to cool her own ardor, and the thought continually penetrated her mind to just pull over and give the woman everything she was pleading for.

The hotel was a lot closer than Rachel's little cottage. The bed had barely been slept in over the few weeks she had been staying there. She really needed to consider sorting out a place of her own, but with the case as hectic as it was right now, she hadn't had time to think about it.

Rachel was giggling and pulling at Sophie's shirt as the detective attempted to slide the keycard into the lock. Sophie grabbed her roughly and shoved her against the wall to the side of the door, holding her in place.

"Wait," Sophie demanded. Her eyes swept over her, and something changed in that moment with the way that Rachel was looking at her. She lost her resolve. Her mouth crashed against Rachel's while her hand continued to manipulate the lock. When it finally clicked open and gave way, she found herself propelled backwards, swiveling on her heels as Rachel took her opportunity.

"You have been on my mind all day," Rachel purred as she finally divested Whitton of her jacket. "I'm attracted to you, Detective, in ways I've never felt before. You make me...hot." She brought her hands up the back of her own neck and lifted her hair, letting it fall as she twirled before falling back against Sophie's chest.

"Really? I can't say I noticed." The dark-haired woman smirked. Rachel's deft fingertips eased each button from its cradle as Sophie watched her intently.

"I need something from you." The shirt was off.

"Yeah? What do you need from me?" The buckle to her belt was slowly tugged loose. Rachel's eyes fixed to the detectives with an intensity that Sophie wasn't used to seeing.

"I need you to stop being so gentle. I know it's in you...let it out," she pleaded, breathy and aroused against Sophie's ear. She bit down gently on the lobe, sucking it between her lips. "I want to feel all that...passion you keep coiled up inside."

~Doll~

The room was dark, curtains drawn. The alcohol coursed through him and left him paralysed in the last place he fell. It was cold on the floor, but the whiskey warmed his being anyway. The nurses would find him eventually, though some part of him hoped maybe they would be too late. He was getting tired, tired of it all.

He'd been doing so well earlier. Just the Bloody Mary for breakfast and a little tipple with his lunch, and then he'd finally opened the post.

Usually the postie only brought brown envelopes stuffed with overdue bills. He would pay them eventually; it just slipped his mind, too consumed with other thoughts. But this time, there had been a different kind of delivery. A pristine white box addressed perfectly to Lord Fenwick.

He liked reading and hearing his full title. Not many people used it now; etiquette had long since gone out of the window. His hands shook, the onset of Parkinson's and the alcohol abuse was now taking its toll. It took a while to pull the lines of cellotape free and then open it. Inside was a parcel covered in bubble wrap. He placed it to one side and pulled the single piece of paper out.

The neat script was instantly recognisable to him as he unfolded the sheet and began to read. All hope of a reconciliation flew out of the window in an instant.

It took a further hour and a half bottle of vodka before he had the courage to unwrap the macabre gift.

A doll, horribly disfigured – and a razor blade with his own name engraved on it.

~Doll~

The detective hovered above her. An ache of immeasurable pleasure clung impatiently to every nerve ending Rachel had. Her detective had had her writhing uncontrollably for almost an hour as she teased and provoked her lover's now naked form. There was nothing she could do to keep the brooding DI from comprehensively taking her apart – not that she wanted to stop her.

She hadn't protested when Sophie had virtually ripped the dress from her body, nor had she complained when the detective followed that up by holding her against the wall and pounding into her. It was a powerful display of hunger and desire, a need to consume and replenish her own vitality. There was no objection either when Rachel found herself on her back and beneath the thrusting core of her lover, her mouth going to work and bringing the detective to her own glorious peak.

This was what she had wanted from the start. The moment she had laid eyes on Whitton, she had seen in her something that most women she met lacked: a desire to get lost in herself, to bring pleasure in her own unique way – not holding back.

Rachel had begged, pleaded, and made promises she knew she would keep if only Sophie would let her climax once more.

Of course, she knew that it would happen. Sophie was not sadistic; she would not leave her wanting.

Chapter Thirty-Two

The office was dark at six in the morning. The only light was the intermittent flickering from the fairy lights on the Christmas tree and the computer screen in front of her. The coffee mug to her left was steaming – too hot to drink and yet she craved it. It would be a miracle if she had managed more than 4 hours of sleep. Her body ached in places she had forgotten existed.

She had left Rachel at the hotel – comatose from the previous night's activity. Coming into the office this early and before anybody else had been an opportunity to let her mind wander over all the jumbled thoughts that were bouncing around inside her head.

By ten to seven, her coffee cup had been drained and Dale Saint had wandered in, flicking the light switches as he entered the room. A dusting of white snowflakes covered his head and shoulders.

"Forget to put 50 pence in the meter?" he asked with a yawn as he pushed his fingers through his hair and shook out the wet icy flakes.

"Nope, just like the dark when I'm still not fully awake." She stood and moved across to the coffee maker. "I'm guessing you'll want one?"

"Do bears shit in the woods?" He took his jacket off, shaking it before hanging it over the back of his chair. "Good night last night, huh?" he asked. He had left the pub when he was told to by Whitton, but not before he'd seen his boss leaving with Rachel.

"I've had worse," she answered, taking a sip of her drink.

"I noticed you and...Rachel..." He left the question unasked. "I wasn't far behind, no idea what time everyone else left." He blushed, his head falling forward as he wished the ground would open up and swallow him whole. "Sorry, none of my business."

One by one the team wandered in and poured themselves coffee. Nobody took a seat; instead they all hovered around their own desks and waited, knowing that whatever Whitton had gotten in her head that meant calling them all in now was going to be important.

She looked around at them all. Eager faces flushed with the coldness outside, rosy cheeks and Rudolph noses. It was hard to imagine any of them had been deliberately trying to undermine the case. She was sure none of them had done that.

"Right, morning," she said, her voice confident and clear. She had their attention now as each one stopped their chitchat and looked her way. "So, this case, as you know, has been under our skin. It's like we're always one step behind the killer." She watched several heads nodding in agreement. "Last night I noticed something, and it got me thinking." She glanced across at Ansu before she continued. "How many of you have gone out after work for a quick pint and got talking about the case?" Nobody said anything, but they each scanned the room looking at one another.

"Come on, nobody is in trouble, I just want to run this by everyone."

Gradually hands raised, and a few of them answered with a quiet, "I have."

"Right, that's what I thought...cos it's what we do, right? We can't leave the job here...we take it with us and keep talking it through." She stood and walked around them all to stand nearer the murder board. "Jeff made a good point earlier: why did he torch the car? How did he know we were looking for it?"

Shrugging shoulders and quizzical faces stared back at her, until one by one it started to dawn on them. "Last night all of us were talking about the case. We treat the pub as though it's an extension of the office."

"Sorry guv," came a couple of voices. She held her palm up.

"It's okay...the point I'm making is this...he uses the Duck. He drinks there."

"Or works there," another voice threw out, and she pointed her finger at him in acknowledgement.

"Or works there, yes. What we need to do now is work out who he is, but it narrows our search." She was animated now. The thought that he was emergency services bothered her, but not half as much as it bothered her not to catch him. He needed to be caught. The psychiatric reports suggested that even when he accomplished whatever it was he was doing, if there was no recognition for his work, he would continue. He was telling them something, and unless they understood it, then he wouldn't stop.

"Andy, I want you to concentrate purely on the staff at the Duck. The rest of you I want checking out the hospital employees, fire service and..." She really didn't like this last bit, but it had to be done. "...anyone here at the station."

There were a lot of disgruntled comments flying back and forth. Nobody wanted to be found looking into colleagues, or worse still, finding out the perp was someone they were working with.

"I don't like it any more than you do...but it has to be done, we can't afford to overlook anyone."

Chapter Thirty-Three

By mid-December, every piece of evidence had been fully checked and tested. Barnard was content to hand over the relevant paperwork. The hair and the tear stain both had the same DNA; they both belonged to the killer. They did not match Gregory Armstrong; that much was clear.

"So, anything else, Doc?" she asked, his office once more the meeting point for updates. She had come alone again, leaving Dale to help go through every single employee at the hospital. Disregarding all female staff, it left them with just under 600 men to do background checks on and compile a list worth looking into further. Bowen and Branson were chasing up fire service personnel, and she had Coleen O'Leary working on the backgrounds of staff at the pub.

"Well, there was one thing, but whether it's related to your case I am not sure?" He sipped his tea as he finished speaking.

"Go on."

"We found a newspaper by the body of Gloria Armstrong." She nodded, remembering the joke about the date. "And we got some fingerprints off of it," he offered.

"Okay, but that would be normal wouldn't it, I mean lots of people probably touched it."

"That is true, the front and back pages you would expect to find more than one print, and that's exactly what we found.

However, inside the paper only two pages were touched, and it was the same finger print on both pages, as though the person had opened the paper specifically to read that story."

"In the system?" she asked hopefully. She could feel the buzz of something important even if she didn't quite know what it was yet.

"Ah, well that's the problem." He smiled, a genuinely disappointed smile. They all wanted this man. "I can tell you that they do not belong to Gloria or Gregory Armstrong." Whitton nodded. "I'll send you copies of the prints."

"Can I get a copy of the entire thing?" she asked, standing as she moved towards the door.

"Of course, I'll have them with you by this afternoon."

~Doll~

The newspaper arrived as promised, along with the documentation relating to the prints and the elimination of Gregory Armstrong from the inquiry. Whitton sat at her desk filling out the relevant paperwork.

"Ma'am?" She looked up to find Andy Bowen standing to the right of her desk. "We're halfway through the brigade, and we've come up with a couple of names. I was thinking, shall I concentrate on these while Jeff carries on with the rest?"

"What's flagged your interest?"

"They've both driven a white Ford at one time or another and, they both lost a kid...I dunno, the doll? I just figured it was worth looking into." He shrugged and sat himself down on the corner of her desk.

"Yeah, look into it. Talk to their chief. Find out who was on shift on the dates in question. Keep it discreet though, huh? I do not want the DCI on our backs cos we've pissed off the brigade."

"Sure thing, Boss." And with that, he was off, calling Branson as he grabbed his jacket and pulled it around his shoulders.

Whitton stretched out and sighed. Her gaze fell on the newspaper again. It had piqued her interest for some reason, so she reached for it. There was a large photograph of a strawberry blonde woman in a hat, smiling as she bent down to a small girl and accepted flowers. The Headline read *Lady Georgina dies suddenly in freak accident.* She remembered the local news being all over it when it happened, something about slipping in the shower. She flicked to pages 4 and 5, the pages that Barnard had marked. It was a continuation of the front page, so she flicked back to that and began to read.

The sudden death of Lady Georgina Fenwick has left the town of Woodington in shock. The 52-year-old ex-socialite turned charitable philanthropist was found in her bathroom early yesterday morning. It is feared she may have slipped on a wet towel, hitting her head as she landed.

Lord Nicholas Fenwick was not available for comment, and his advisors have asked for privacy for the family during this time.

Read on for our tribute on pages 4 and 5.

"Here ya go. One cup of milky coffee with an extra shot and two sugars. Just the way ya like it." Dale smiled as he placed the cardboard takeaway cup on the desk in front of her. "*And* just because you're my favourite DI, a mince pie!" He placed a small bag down next to the cup. She squinted up at him as she folded her arms, trying to read the smile that was still plastered to his face.

"What do you want?" she asked. Assuming he was after something, she placed the newspaper back down on the desk.

"What? I can't pick you up a coffee and a treat when I'm visiting Costa?" he asked, his voice an octave higher than usual.

"Every morning we take turns to buy the coffee, this morning was my turn and I supplied the goods...so, what are you after?"

He laughed and held his hands up in surrender. "I am not after anything, Becky is..." When Whitton sat silently awaiting the rest of it, he reluctantly continued. "She wanted to invite you...and, uh...Rachel to dinner. I said it wasn't..."

She cut him off with a raised palm. "I'll ask her." She wasn't sure why she was half-agreeing to this. Obviously Rachel could just say no and that would be the end of it, though she doubted she would turn down the opportunity. It was all too soon really, but what the hell, she had been fucking up her love life for months – why stop now?

"You'll...okay, so I'll wait...Okay."

"Okay?"

"Yes..." He turned to leave and then stopped. "I know it's none of my business, but I'm going to say it anyway." He checked to make sure nobody else was listening. "Whatever you and Rachel have got going on, well it suits you...you seem more...happier lately. "

"Right, well thanks for that, now do you have something to do or do I need to find you something?" He grinned and turned away. She smiled and picked up her coffee, peeking inside the bag. "And a mince pie," she mumbled to herself gleefully.

Chapter Thirty-Four

Outside it was arctic. The northerly wind was bitterly cold as Sophie pulled the car into the kerb outside of Dale and Becky's home. It was warm and toasty inside the vehicle, helped by the fact that Rachel was wearing a dress that had sent Sophie's temperature rising.

The blonde nurse had really gone to town in making an effort to impress, much to Sophie's amusement. She had barely managed to change her shirt before picking Rachel up, but her date knew how to dress. Her dress was petrol blue and fell just above her knees. It was long-sleeved and cut just low enough to give a peek of the voluptuousness that hid beneath it.

She sat fidgeting in her seat, smoothing invisible creases away from her lap.

"What's the matter?" Sophie asked softly. She twisted in her seat as she yanked the handbrake up and switched off the ignition.

"Nothing..." Rachel answered, smiling nervously. "Okay, I'm shitting it...this is like..." She breathed deeply and exhaled slowly. "This is...before we were just fucking and now, our colleagues are waiting for us to join them for dinner." She looked out of the window towards the flat. She held up the carrier bag she'd been holding on her lap. "We've even bought their kids Christmas presents."

"Oh...and you'd prefer to just keep fucking?" Her serious tone caused Rachel to turn around quickly. "Because, we can cancel if you've changed your mind."

"No... that's not..." She reached out for Sophie's hand and held it between her own. "I just think maybe we should clarify what we are."

"I see. What do you want us to be?"

"That's not fair..."

"Rachel, last time we broached this you said you was a big girl and it was what it was...if that's changed then yeah, maybe we need to talk about it." They held each other's gaze for a moment as each of them considered what they wanted.

"I want to talk about it," she whispered.

"Okay." Sophie reached for the key to re-engage the engine.

"What are you doing?" The question caught Sophie off guard. "We can't not go in," Rachel stated. "That would be rude. Look, I just need to know how to act."

"What do you mean 'how to act?'"

"For a detective, you can be very obtuse at times!" She grinned. "Right now, all I want to do is touch you. Can I do that? Are you going to be comfortable with me being tactile with you in front of others?" Her fingers reached out instinctively. Sophie felt the shiver that always made its way down her spine, and it had nothing to do with the weather outside; it was always Rachel. She felt herself nodding.

"Rachel, honestly I dunno what we are or if this is going to last or what, but I'm not hiding you. I'm not ashamed of our relationship and clearly, having been invited, you're not a secret." She leant across the car and kissed her. "We're just having dinner with our friends and then we'll go back to yours and I can come in or go, whatever you decide."

~Doll~

Harry and Ella were running around the living room like the vicious wind outside, only these two little monkeys were warm and cute and doing no harm other than driving their parents to distraction.

Sophie had been a guest here a few times, mainly late into the evening when eating had been a last-minute plan and Becky had sent a text demanding that Dale get home before she started her shift. Dinner would be provided, and the two of them would sit at the kitchen table with their notes and talk things through.

For Rachel, it was a first. She hadn't been working at Woodington University Hospital that long, and Becky was the first person to befriend her. Not that she wasn't a sociable and outgoing person, because she was, she had no trouble finding people to spend time with, but it was fair to say that Becky and herself had developed a closer friendship at work. It was nice to now take that out of hours, even if it was a little awkward.

She knew that Becky hadn't been happy with her for pursuing the detective and she understood why: Becky was loyal to a relationship. For her there was a rulebook and you didn't break it; for Rachel, those rules were for other people.

"Come on Harry, get down from Auntie Sophie." Dale attempted to grab his mischievous daughter from Sophie's back, but the Detective twisted away and both of them giggled. "Not helping!" he said, trying not to smile at the pair of them.

"Why don't I take the munchkin to bed?" Sophie said, hoisting the little blonde-haired girl higher up her back. "Come on Trouble, Ella Bella you too." She reached her hand out to the other blonde-haired bundle of excitement. "Time for bed."

The other three adults in the room watched as Sophie and the kids left the room. It felt a little awkward as Dale considered what to do or say next. Becky saved his blushes.

"Dale, table needs laying," she ordered. Turning to Rachel, she smiled. "Dinner won't be long. The kids were supposed to be with my mum tonight but she had to cancel last minute, so they've had chicken nuggets and chips already."

"Great, they're cute kids," Rachel replied. She still held the bottle of wine in her hand. "Oh, this is for you," she said, handing it over. Becky took the bottle and examined the label as though she were a fine wine critic. Placing it in the fridge, she spoke again.

"So, how's things going with you two..." She pulled a cold bottle of wine from the shelf and closed the door. When she turned back around, her eyes landed directly on Rachel with an intense stare.

"Actually, I think it's going well. We uh, it's a day-by-day thing really." She blushed as she considered why it was that Becky was looking at her that way. "Look, I know that you...I know what you think of this and...of me, but it is what it is, and we both know what we're doing."

"Do you?" she hissed, trying to keep her voice down. She checked on the saucepan. Water was bubbling up and spitting as it waited – she knew how it felt. "You split them up."

"No, I didn't, and to be honest, it's none of your business, Becks." She kept calm. This was supposed to be an enjoyable evening with friends. "Look, maybe this is a bad idea...do you want me to just go?"

"No, you're right, it's none of my business...I just-" Becky sighed and threw the pasta in the pan. "I don't want to see either of you get hurt. Sophie is...God, she's surly and brash, gives off this whole badass, nothing-gets-to-me image, but she's not like that..." She had moved across the kitchen and now stood facing Rachel, a friendly standoff. "Beneath that surface she's...she's deep, and just when you think you've worked her out, she surprises you."

"I know that. Why do you think I am attracted to her? I know you think I don't know what I'm doing, but I do...I know what I like, and I like her."

"Okay."

"Okay?"

"Yeah, come on, let's eat, shall we?" Becky smiled and placed her arm around Rachel's shoulder and led them both to the dining room.

Chapter Thirty-Five

Finally, the time had come. He had waited long enough, and now, he had found him. It couldn't have worked out any better really. The hours of watching and waiting were beginning to take their toll, and he hadn't been sure if he would be able to complete his mission, but then there he was, right in front of him.

He was perfect.

Not having a vehicle anymore had been an issue. He had wanted to replace the car, but he didn't want to draw attention to the fact that he had gotten rid of the other one. But, in the end it didn't matter because the one he had chosen had a car, and he was too drunk to drive himself home, even though he had every intention of doing just that. That was when he realised that this was the right man.

He didn't take him home however; instead he took him to the place where he needed to leave his message.

He had spent all evening watching as he stumbled around from the bar to the toilets and back again, a small piss stain getting larger with each visit. He was a walking disgrace, only interested in his own ability to get another whisky. He stank, and looking at him just made his blood curdle.

It was dark, pitch black without the headlights. The wind swirled in all directions. Winter had well and truly arrived. He shivered; not just from the cold that took his breath away with every suck of air into his lungs, but from the prospect of almost completing his mission. Once this message had been left for the world to see, he would have one thing left to do, and then it would be complete. Then he would be free of it, free of them all.

In the passenger seat, strapped into the seatbelt, was the snoring, dribbling figure of his next message. They'd been parked up for a few minutes while he went through in his mind everything that he needed to do. Christmas songs played merrily in the background on the radio. Humming along, he reached back into the car for the small rucksack he carried. Unzipping it, he fumbled inside and found what he would need and felt the weight of it in his hand as he contemplated just what he planned to do with it. It wasn't something he would enjoy, but needs must. He had to show everyone.

Taking a deep breath, he opened the driver's door and stepped out into the fresh snow. It was coming down again, big flakes of pure white. He thought of Tiffany. He never knew what happened, really. One minute she was there and the next she was gone. They said she had died in her sleep, peacefully by her own hand. But when he had asked to see her, they wouldn't let him. He was seven years old. He had gone to her room, without their knowledge he had sneaked in there. Everything was just how it should be. Her silk pajamas were folded neatly on her pillow, but someone had placed the Doll on top of it. He had touched it, reached out a tiny hand and ran his finger down its center. His mother caught him, shouted at him, and he had run from the room and out of the house, into the snow.

Trudging around the front of the car, he slipped and found himself laughing, remembering the day when Tiffany had shoved him over and they had both landed on their backs and made angels. His face flushed with the anger of it all. Grabbing the passenger door, he yanked it open and leaned inside. The stench of stale breath, alcohol, and an unkempt human being was enough to make him gag, but he got control of himself and unbuckled the seatbelt.

The man's head lolled from side to side, still drunk as he mumbled incoherently about the cold and another whiskey. Pulling on his jacket, he jerked him sideways and pulled him from the car. He landed in a heap on his knees, tried to stagger to his feet. Pathetic really.

He didn't really feel the first blow as his head whipped back and bounced off the side of the car, or the next that pushed him face first into the snow and mud. By the time he was sitting in the driver's seat, he had been dead for twenty minutes, and a lone figure walked briskly along the country lane that headed back into town.

Chapter Thirty-Six

Dinner had ended on a happy note. Becky and Rachel had polished off a bottle of wine between them, and then gone on to finish what was left of the one that Dale and Sophie had each enjoyed a glass of. Being on the job, and involved in a case like the Doll Maker, meant that they wanted to keep clear heads, just in case something broke.

Sophie helped Rachel with her coat, then shrugging her own on, thanked their hosts for a wonderful evening, making promises to do something similar again soon. And it had been a nice night. Conversation had flowed back and forth, sticking to safer subjects. Nobody mentioned work at all.

The car was covered in an inch of freshly laid snow already. Streetlamps cast an eerie yellow glow across the white expanse. The only sound was footsteps from Sophie and Rachel, leading from the house along the pavement. Rachel shivered, hugging herself as Sophie began to swipe the snow free from the windscreen with her arm.

"Get in the car," Sophie all but ordered. It didn't make sense that both of them remained cold. She put the key in the ignition and started the engine. Reaching inside, she turned the heater dial around to its hottest setting. "Rachel?"

"Sorry, what?" She shook herself from her thoughts, flakes of snow falling from her hair and coat like tiny particles of stardust.

"I said, get in the car, no point both of us being cold." Sophie held the door open for her and waited until she was safely ensconced. It didn't take much longer to clear the glass, and then she herself jumped in, blowing into her hands to warm them. "Okay?"

"Yeah, cold, isn't it? This snow looks like it's in for the night too," she noted, glancing out of the now steaming-up window and up at the night sky. It wasn't that late, but the street was quiet, like the world had looked outside and declined to venture out. "Reminds me of the night I left home."

"Where was home?" Sophie asked. She hadn't noticed any particular accent in Rachel's voice. She spoke nicely, like most women who had attended University did, but there was no specific twang in her intonation.

"Actually, here," she said, looking out of the window as the flakes fell. "I'm from Woodington originally." Her voice fell flat; saddened by memories maybe.

"Really, I didn't expect that. So, you left here and went where?" The snow was coming down thick and fast now. She flicked the window wipers up and watched as they sped up, wiping the snow away only for it to be replaced in an instant.

"Manchester and then Sheffield. Cities to get lost in."

"What brought you back?" Sophie kept her eyes on the road ahead. It was darker as they neared Rachel's cottage, and the street lamps became further apart.

"Are you interrogating me, Detective?" She smiled, but there was a defiance behind her eyes. She didn't want to keep answering these questions.

"No, just interested," Sophie answered. She took her eyes off of the road for a second to glance at Rachel. Their eyes fell on each other. "*You* interest me, okay?"

Rachel thought for a moment before reaching out and placing her hand over Sophie's as it rested on the gearstick. "I missed it, I guess. I'd been away for over fifteen years, and I wanted to settle down. After Uni, I spent time traveling from job to job, escaping my past. Eventually, I realised that what I needed was some counselling." Sophie listened intently. "It helped a lot. I found that once I got everything out and worked my way through it, that it was easier to contemplate moving home."

"Well, I am glad, and your family must be too."

"Doubtful." She smiled sadly, and Sophie took that as her cue to drop it.

The drive back to Rachel's was slow and laborious with all the hazards that ice and snow can bring. Barely getting above twenty miles per hour, Sophie used to the time to contemplate. Her head was awash with thoughts. The case was always on her mind, questions she needed to remind herself to find answers to the following day, but mainly her love life seemed to be at the forefront of her mind lately. It bothered her a little that she hadn't even thought about Yvonne these past few weeks. In fact, her mind, when not at work, had been solely occupied with thoughts of the woman sitting next to her, a woman that she now knew a little more about. She chanced a quick glance at her and smiled. Rachel had reclined the seat and was now quietly singing along to the Christmas song playing on the radio. Her eyes were closed, and she was relaxed and smiling. She looked breathtaking. Without thinking, Sophie reached out her left hand and placed it gently atop Rachel's thigh. There was something more intimate now about their relationship – sex was great, but it was more than that, an intimacy she had lost somewhere along the way with Yvonne. Rachel sighed contentedly and placed her own hand back on top of Sophie's, entwining their fingers.

Sophie pulled the car into the kerb outside of Rachel's cottage and left the engine running. She had to move her hand away from Rachel in order to yank the handbrake up, and she felt the loss instantly. Rachel flipped the lever and her seat rose up. "Are you coming in?"

"Do you want me to?" she asked, hope lingering with each syllable. Rachel leant forwards and pressed her lips firmly against Sophie's.

"Hmm mmm," she murmured before deepening the kiss.

Chapter Thirty-Seven

Coldness seeped into Whitton's bones as she stood on the verge of the country lane, either side closed off to traffic with blue and white tape. It was gone 3 a.m. and eerily quiet. Police cars and two ambulances blocked the road with blue lights flashing and bouncing off of the blanket of white that had settled across the fields. Each leaf, twig, and branch was covered in a fine layer that would steadily build until the weight of it forced it to fall to the ground.

Barnard's minions were also milling around doing what they were paid to do: collecting and cataloguing all of the evidence.

When the call had come in, it hadn't been that long since she had fallen asleep. Having to leave Rachel warm under the duvet and head outside where Dale was waiting, the engine ticking over to keep the heat, was not how she imagined her night would end. She had been so warm and comfortable pressed up against Rachel's skin.

Fumes from the exhaust had created a cloud of white smoke in the darkness that swirled like a ghostly figure behind the car. Her feet crunched with every step as she trod through virgin snow along the path. Flinging the door open, she hopped in quickly, leaving the cold behind for a little while.

"Another bloke?" she had said. There had been very few details other than she was required to go to a scene out on Cruikshank lane.

They watched as the little white suits moved around the car that was the center of everybody's attention, blending in with the backdrop of snow-covered bushes and trees. The lighting was being kept to a minimum. Footsteps in the snow and mud needed to be recorded before the heat from any industrial bulbs melted the evidence.

The car was a nice one: a Mercedes E-Class. It belonged to a man whose body they assumed was sitting in the driver's seat. Of course, they would need to get confirmation of that, but right now Mr James Frasier was looking very much like the latest victim of the Doll Maker.

"James Frasier, 52 years old from Woodington. We've got a business card in his wallet. He was an accountant. I've got uniform going round now to the address to let next of kin know," Dale explained. "Hands have been glued, gripping the steering wheel." He grimaced. "He's taken a beating with something heavy, a hammer possibly."

"Delightful," Whitton said, her voice steady and calm.

"That's not all though, the doll. He glued it to a bottle of vodka by the hands," Dale explained. "And he stinks like a brewery."

"Why did he do it here?" she asked, speaking to herself more than anyone else. The question had been bouncing around in her mind since they got here. It was the middle of nowhere. The only reason it had been found so quickly was because an ambulance had visited the nursing home further up the road. They had passed the car on their way and not taken much notice of it, assuming someone had broken down. When it was still there on their return 45 minutes later, they stopped to offer assistance; it wasn't a night to be stuck on the roadside. Instead, what they had found was the badly beaten and butchered body of a male in his 50s.

"You're asking me? This guy is a lunatic, who knows," Dale replied. "Maybe he waved him over and stopped him here?"

"Seat's all wrong." At Dale's quizzical look, she added, "Look at the position of the victim, the seat's too far back. He couldn't have driven. Someone with longer legs drove, and someone with long legs could never have sat in the passenger seat, look how far forward it is. The last person that sat there was also shorter."

"I wouldn't have noticed that," he admitted.

"It means something." She looked around them. There was nothing here. He could have taken him anywhere: gone home with him, done it where he met him, but he hadn't. Instead, he had driven him and stopped here, in this quiet country lane. "This place, there is a reason for it. We just need to work out what it is."

The two-man ambulance crew were sitting in the back of their own ambulance while their colleagues checked them out for shock. It was one thing being prepared for the scene of an accident; it was something completely different to come across a victim of the Doll Maker. Sophie wandered across and hung back while the medics did their job. Once they finished, she moved in. She recognised them both. Medics and cops often came into contact with each other. She had no idea of their names without being told by the first officer on the scene, but she knew they would know who she was.

"Alright?" She nodded at them as they looked her way.

"Yeah, bit shook up, ya know?" the one she now knew was Matt Chivers answered. "We see a lot of, ya know, bad stuff... we figured it was just a broken down car."

"Yeah, I can imagine it wasn't fun," Sophie agreed. "I'm gonna need a statement from you both. I was told you was returning from a call out to Branford?"

"We were." This time it was Derek Fargo that answered. "Patient fell over. Banged himself up a bit and was on the floor for a while until one of the nurses found him. Third time this year for us." He curled his hand and made a drinking motion with it. "Too many sherbets."

Sophie smiled. She got the message. "So, how long was you up there for?"

"About forty minutes. We got him upright and checked him over. He was ok, few bruises but nothing broken," Derek answered. "We got the call just after eleven thirty. It took us about 20 minutes to get over here, so we passed the car around eleven fifty?" He glanced at his colleague for corroboration.

"Yeah, the car was there. Its lights were on, but the engine wasn't."

"Did you notice anyone else in the car?" They both shook their heads.

"No, wasn't paying that much attention to it to be honest. We had enough issues with the weather and watching out for black ice, but ya notice things like lights and obstacles," Derek said, while Matt nodded.

"So, you left your patient around twelve thirty?" Sophie asked, getting the timeline straight in her mind.

"Hang on, it's on the paperwork." Derek was the older of the two, but he jumped down from the back of the vehicle and quickly grabbed his clipboard from the front seat. Back in seconds, he continued. "Arrived 23:57, departed 00:33."

Sophie jotted it down. "And then you found the driver in the car?" Derek nodded.

"Yeah. Oh, what about that bloke?" Matt said, looking towards his partner. "He was walking along the lane towards Woodington. He might have passed the car too."

"Or left the car?" Sophie mumbled. "I need those statements as soon as possible."

Chapter Thirty-Eight

The conference room was warmer now that ten bodies filled the seats around the oak veneer table. Each of them had a cup of tea or coffee, except for Colleen O'Leary, who preferred a fresh orange juice.

They were using the privacy of the conference room in order to eliminate any potential sharing of information. Whitton was insistent now that they were close. All it would take was one lead, one link, and they would be bearing down on the Doll Maker and bringing his murder spree to an end.

"Jeff, tell me about the brigade," she said, sipping her coffee as she swiveled in her chair to face him.

"Well, Andy and I talked with the watch commander. They've got two guys, Banning and Higgins. Both of them were off work on the nights of the first two victims. However, on the night Bancroft was murdered, Banning was working a 12-hour shift and Higgins was visiting family in Jamaica." He shrugged and picked up his coffee. "Other than that, nothing stood out."

"Good, that rules them out, and we can put the brigade to one side for now. Colleen?"

Colleen looked up at her boss and nodded. Standing, she walked quickly across the room to the white board.

"So, I spent a lot of time on this. I started off with 586 men that work at the hospital, either employed or as volunteers. Via HR

I was able to remove 347 instantly as being on shift during at least one of the murders." She wrote the numbers on the board. "Another 235 were on annual leave or rest days during the...."

"Murders, yeah we get it," laughed Ansu Patel.

"Yes, and mostly they're either too old, not Caucasians, and not redheads or bleached blondes," Colleen continued. "So that left me with 4 potential suspects." Everybody in the room sat up and paid attention. "These 4 were not at work for all three of the original victims." She then added a photograph and wrote the name beneath. "And this guy, Noel Edward Sanders. He was off work for all of those dates, and the night of James Frasier he called in sick, *and* he is a redhead."

"What about Gary Price?"

"Here's where it gets good. He goes to college with Gary Price. He was there that day."

"Are you serious?" Whitton asked, sitting forward in her seat. "Okay, I want a full rundown on this guy." Several people stood to leave. "Hang on, we're not done. I'm not placing all our eggs into one basket until we have exhausted every other option. Dale, what about here?" The team sat back down in their seats and gave Saint their attention.

"I have to say that I wasn't particularly keen on doing this, but I have, and I can honestly say that there isn't anyone that stands out. But, I am still going through some details so, I will update as soon as I can."

"Alright. Ansu, what have ya got from the pub?"

"Tony. I have to say that guy gives me the creeps." He rubbed the back of his neck. "There are only 8 people on staff there currently, but over the past year they have had 23. I've been through them all and only Tony stands out as the oddball."

"Dates? Was he working during the times these girls were killed?"

"Hard to say, they don't keep a track of rotas. Once the week is over and the staff have been paid – out of the till by the way – they toss the rota and put the new one up."

"Okay, add his name to the board." She sipped her coffee some more and focused on the board as Ansu added the name to that of Noel Sanders. "Fenwick? Why do I know that name?" She began rifling through the paperwork in front of her, flicking between statements and copies of files from Barnard. "Here!" she pulled out the copy of the newspaper found at the scene where Gloria Armstrong was murdered. "Lady Fenwick died a few days before Gloria."

"Did we just find our trigger?"

Chapter Thirty-Nine

Whitton had divided the team into two groups. Dale Saint took charge of the Sanders investigation, whilst Jeff Branson got the investigation under way regarding Tony Fenwick.

Either man could be their killer. Whitton wasn't going to be quick to judgement just yet, but she was leaning towards Tony Fenwick; they just had no real evidence. Hunches only took you so far, and they needed to build a solid case. For now, they needed more than just circumstantial evidence and gut feelings.

The rest of the article had been interesting. According to the reporter, Lord and Lady Fenwick had been devoted to each other from the day they met. Marrying quickly in 1983, the two socialites had set the social scene alight with their love affair. Many expected that they would leave the social scene behind them, but in fact they had become even more embroiled in nights out, often caught by paparazzi as they moved from one venue to the next. There were rumours of drug-taking and alcohol-fueled romps, but nobody ever clarified or denied.

Two years into the marriage, Georgina Fenwick was pregnant. Once again, it was assumed they would break from the scene. Tiffany was born healthy in 1985, but the young soon-to-be Lady Fenwick assumed her place with Nicholas on many a night out. The baby was taken care of by nannies.

At some point, Georgina Fenwick had slowly taken a step back. Nicholas, however, only seemed more encouraged to avoid family life and continue to party. It wasn't until a second child, Anthony, arrived over ten years later that Nicholas too began to show signs of growing up. Becoming a father for the second time had clearly made an impression.

Sadly, Lord Fenwick, as he had since become, found life difficult and was subsequently arrested for drunk driving, twice. A fine and slap on the wrist, though, seemed to settle him down again.

The family were involved in a serious car accident in the summer of 1997 when Lady Fenwick was driving the family home from a party. While navigating Cruickshank Lane, the car veered off and hit a verge, flipping the car onto its side. Lord and Lady Fenwick suffered only minor injuries. However, the children had not been so lucky. Neither had been strapped into seatbelts as they were both sleeping on the backseat.

Tiffany suffered a broken arm and needed an emergency operation to remove her spleen, while the younger child, Anthony had a severe concussion and a broken leg.

There wasn't much else to the story other than that nothing further was known about Tiffany, once she left home to study. The youngster had managed to keep away from the limelight for the most part, and the press had agreed not to write anything further about young Anthony.

"Cruickshank Lane and a missing spleen," Sophie muttered to herself. "Now it's all starting to fall into place."

~Doll~

Whitton parked the car and climbed out. O'Leary was with her and followed suit. It was still snowing, and she pulled her jacket around herself and zipped it up as they walked the pavement back towards the house she wanted to visit.

"I bet he ain't too pleased to see us," O'Leary said, wiping her nose with a tissue that she shoved back inside her pocket.

"Probably not," Whitton agreed, her features impassive. She wasn't in the mood to play lip service today.

The scruffy front garden looked a little bit less of a mess under the weight of all the snow. Winter always seemed to make everything look just that little bit more beautiful. O'Leary reached for the knocker and gave it two loud bangs against the paint-flaked wood, and waited.

Gregory Armstrong looked a mess when he opened the door. His bleached hair, now showing ginger roots, was unkempt and stuck out at all angles. His face was gaunt, and he looked as though he hadn't slept in days.

"What do you want?" His voice was gruff and angry. He held the door open, but kept his body in the way.

"Just a quick chat, Gregory." Whitton smiled and took a step forwards.

"It's still Pete." He rolled his eyes at her, but stepped aside, sniffing loudly as she passed him. He followed them down the short hallway and into the living room. Empty pizza boxes and beer cans littered the table in front of the couch. Clearly he hadn't been keeping up on his cleaning.

"*Pete*, I need to ask you a question."

"Like I can stop ya," he moaned. Picking up a cushion, he tossed it to the floor, the threadbare carpet catching it perfectly. He flopped down into the space left by the cushion and looked up at her expectantly.

"The last time you saw your..." She noticed the grimace on his face and changed tact. "Gloria, did she have anyone hanging around?"

"You mean shagging someone or pimping them out?"

"Either...does anyone stick out in your mind as being around a lot?" she pressed him, needing a name.

"I guess," he answered. She stared him down for a moment and waited. "There was always someone hanging about. Filthy old perverts and the like, but yeah, she had someone."

"You got a name?"

"I dunno why I should bother helping you out. Look at me, no job. Me mates are steering clear..."

"I need a name, Pete." She ignored his little rant. Of course his life had turned to shit. He was on bail for a possible murder. "I need a name, you need to give me a name if you want to clear yourself from this Doll Maker bollox."

That got his attention. Right now, regardless of the evidence, he was the man the police had talked to about the Doll Maker Murders. Rumours were rife, and they all revolved around Peter Wilson.

"Tony. I dunno his last name, he was hanging around for years. She had him working, but they were fucking too."

"Where can I find this Tony?" She needed to be sure that it was the same man, dot all the I's and cross all the T's.

"He works down the pub now, at the Duck."

It really wasn't looking good for Anthony Fenwick; everything was now pointing in his direction, but proving that he was in fact the killer wasn't that simple. They needed more if they were to get a warrant to arrest him and take DNA samples, but not much more – they were close!

Chapter Forty

Woodington town centre was awash with partygoers and those still hunting down a bargain while the shops endured a late-night opening. Revelers strolled from bar to club and back again on countless Christmas parties, staggering more easily as the night wore on.

Windows that welcomed in passersby with flashing lights and displays built to entice and encourage men and women alike to part with their well-earned cash. Rachel waited just inside one, in one of the nicer restaurants in town. Her table for two held a lit candle, a menu on each side, and a couple of wine glasses waiting to be filled. She perused her menu as she waited, and occasionally her eyes rose up and glanced out of the steamed window in the hope of seeing Sophie. The waiter arrived with the bottle of red that she had ordered and poured her a glass.

Arriving early, she wasn't too worried that Sophie hadn't got there yet, but it was nearing the hour already, and the detective was still nowhere to be seen. She would give it fifteen more minutes though.

The wine was very nice. She was on her second glass when the door finally opened and her detective strolled inside. *Her detective.* She wondered to herself just how long she had been considering Sophie Whitton as hers. Snow fell from the mop of short hair that hung loose from underneath the hoodie Sophie wore. She looked exhausted.

"Sorry, I got held up," she explained. Shrugging her jacket off, she draped it across the back of her chair and leant across to place a soft kiss on Rachel's cheek. Her skin was warm, no doubt from the heating within the car.

"That's okay. You look tired, are you sure you want to stay?" Rachel asked. Reaching across the table, she placed her hand over Sophie's. "I don't mind, we can go back to mine and order a pizza." She smiled.

"That sounds delightful, but not tonight." Sophie reached for the bottle with her free hand and poured herself a good glug. "To us, and our first proper date," she said, raising the glass.

"To us." Their glasses clinked as they both smiled. A new understanding had developed over the last few days. Since the dinner party at Dale's, things had progressed quite comfortably, so much so that Sophie hadn't thought twice when Rachel had suggested a date. It made perfect sense. Whether it was sensible was another matter, but right now, Rachel was what she needed.

"So, how was your day?" Sophie asked. The starter had arrived, and she hadn't realised just how famished she actually was.

"Oh, you know, the usual. It's Christmas, so lots of people doing stupid things and ending up in a theatre being patched up. You?"

Sophie put her fork down and took a swig from her wine glass. She glanced around the room. Those closest to them were too busy enjoying themselves to pay any attention to anything Sophie was saying. She leant forward and whispered, "I think we've got him."

"What? Really?" Sophie nodded and grinned. "Who?" She immediately shook her head. "No, sorry, I know you can't say, but... wow, that's awesome!"

"Yeah, Dale is putting everything together so I can take it to the magistrate tomorrow. Half the team are staking him out, I'll have to go in really early."

"That's okay, we can just enjoy dinner and call it a night."

~Doll~

Calling it a night meant going back to Rachel's and falling into bed. Sophie was too wired to sleep anyway. Tomorrow was going to be a big day – huge!

Rachel could sense the edginess within her, just the same as she had that first night they slept together. The detective fell backwards onto the bed with Rachel astride her lap, deftly unbuttoning her shirt. She didn't speak. There was no need for words, although she had plenty she wanted to say. Sophie's eyes darkened as she watched her, nimble fingers making light work of the fiddly little white buttons. Rachel slid her palms under the opening and pushed the shirt open. Braless, Sophie felt soft palms stroke across her nipples. Her back arched and she wanted nothing more than to take control, but she wouldn't, for now. For some reason still unknown to her, she liked letting Rachel take charge. Maybe it was because there was no force to it. Rachel didn't *need* to be in control; she took charge to bring relief, pleasure, and to release the tension that built up within her.

Tonight was one of those nights.

When soft lips encased her nipple and a gentle tongue swept around it decisively, it was all Sophie could do not to cry out. Her eyes were fixed on her lover, but she could feel the smile on Rachel's lips; it mirrored her own. She let her own palms slide back and forth along Rachel's thighs, squeezing the flesh as she glided upwards to take two more handfuls of soft flesh within her palms.

"You are completely overdressed," she quipped. "Take it off."

Rachel stopped kissing her throat and sat up, grinding herself hard against her lover's abdomen. She grasped the hem of her top and lifted, revealing bra-clad breasts to the watching detective below her. "Better?" she grinned.

"A little. Bra next." Her order was simple and clear. "I wanna see you."

"You do see me. That much I am very sure of," Rachel replied, leaning forward to capture lips with her own. When she sat back up, her bra fell from her shoulders and she tossed it aside.

"Nice." Sophie grinned. "Now, the rest."

Rachel smiled, placed her hands against Sophie's chest, and leant forward once more. "Why don't you help me with that?" She lifted her backside and smirked as she felt Sophie's fingers hook into her pants and slide them over her arse. Within seconds, she was on her back with Sophie yanking the offending clothes from her legs.

"Now, that's better." The way she looked at Rachel now was salacious. She wasted no time in taking her with her mouth, bringing her arms around soft thighs and holding her in place. She would enjoy this just as much as Rachel would.

"Yeah, that is better," Rachel managed before all of her linguistic skills abandoned her and all that was left were whimpers and pleas.

Chapter Forty-One

Noel Sanders was officially eliminated when it was confirmed that he didn't live in or near Woodington when Gloria Armstrong had been murdered. He had been working 300 miles away in a nursing home.

Now, their only suspect was Anthony Fenwick. His photograph was stuck to the center of the murder board, his name emblazoned in large capital letters across the top. All the details they had on him were scribbled down the left and right side of the picture.

Tony the barman was a man with a shaved head in his twenties. Anthony Fenwick's university identity card showed a completely different character. A little younger, clean shaven, but with a mop of red hair. Speaking to the bar manager, it was also noted that he had started the job as a redhead, but had then bleached it blonde. However, he had shaved it all off completely a few weeks ago.

Alongside his photograph were the photographs of Gloria Armstrong, Sandra Bancroft, Anjelika Tyszka, and Emma Taylor, along with Gary Price and James Frasier as they were in life and death. Beneath those photographs were the images of Lady and Lord Fenwick. Beneath those photographs were several more images, this time depicting each doll.

"What have we got? Run it by me," Whitton called out to the room. She sat at her desk with her feet up and her arms behind her head. She looked like the epitome of relaxation to anyone else observing her, but like the proverbial duck, underneath it all she was flapping, desperate to get this guy locked up before the day was out.

"He is a redhead." Dale shouted out the obvious.

"He was the owner of a white Ford Focus." Patel waved a piece of paper with the DVLA logo on it.

"And we have a witness that puts him in Gloria's life at the same time his mother died," Whitton added, dropping her feet to the floor.

"The accident, when he was a kid..." Colleen spoke up now. "Cruickshank Lane. I went back over records, and James Frasier was left in pretty much the exact spot of the accident."

"Okay, it's all good. It all links him, but..."

"Ma'am?" a voice shouted out across the room. "Someone to see you." Sophie looked up and found Andy Bowen pointing to Rachel. She looked white as a sheet, her gazed fixed on the murder board. It wasn't pretty, the shots of dead people like that. Even as a nurse and dealing with the dead and dying, it wasn't quite the same as seeing the body of a murder victim.

"Okay, take a break. Dale, get me a coffee?" she asked as she moved quickly towards Rachel. Leading her by the elbow, she tried to draw her away, but Rachel resisted and moved towards the board. "Hey, come on...you don't need to see that."

"You left your phone." Her voice sounded numb. She was holding out the mobile without looking at Sophie. "Is that him?" She continued to stare.

"Yeah, look you can't be in here." Sophie tried again to lead her out of the conference room and back into the office.

"Sophie, I...we need to talk." Finally her eyes left the photographs and came to rest on her lover.

"Can it wait? Rachel, I'm in the middle of something huge here." She raked her hand through her hair. If she was going to get dumped, then it wasn't going to be in the middle of her fucking office surrounded by her colleagues.

"No, I don't think it can, Sophie." Her eyes were wet with tears, and she looked as though she might pass out. "Why are my parents' photographs on that board?" Sophie's head swiveled to look at the board and then back again at Rachel.

"What do you mean?"

"My parents, you have my parents' photographs on your board. Why?"

"Okay, come with me." She put an arm around her and led her urgently towards a small empty office. Once inside and away from prying eyes and listening ears, she locked the door. She pulled a chair out and helped her lower into the chair. ""Sit. Now, breathe and tell me what's going on."

Before Rachel could speak, there was a gentle tapping on the door. Sophie stood quickly and yanked it open to find Dale holding out two mugs of coffee.

"Thanks. Can you take over for a minute? I just need to..." She looked over her shoulder at Rachel. "I won't be long, okay?"

"Sure Sophie, take ya time. I'm on it. Fenwick won't know what's hit him." At the mention of the name Rachel began to sniff, fighting the urge to sob. Her breath was ragged as she gulped for air.

Sophie closed the door again and placed the coffee on the desk. Kneeling in front of Rachel, she took hold of her hands and waited, unsure quite where to start.

"Tell me what's upsetting you? What do you mean 'your parents are on the board?'" Sophie probed gently. She couldn't imagine Gloria Armstrong or James Frasier were related to Rachel, though it would make sense why she had run at the earliest opportunity if Gloria had had anything to do with her life.

"Fuck, I didn't want to tell you like this..." She wiped her face with the back of her hand, streaks of black mascara marking them and her cheeks. "Sophie..." She reached out and cupped the detective's cheek. Taking a deep breath, she exhaled and then explained. "My name isn't Rachel. I mean, legally it is. I changed it when I left home, a new start away from everything and everyone I knew." Sophie stood. Her knees ached, and so she perched her backside on the edge of the desk and continued to listen. "My parents, well you wouldn't really give them that title, they did so little parenting...My mother tried to make amends, when she discovered what her own brother was up to every time he babysat for us so they could go out, but it was too late by then." Sophie rubbed a palm over her face as she imagined a young Rachel being mistreated by the very people that should have protected her. "When I was 17, I told my mother that she either help me to leave or I would go to the newspapers. The scandal would have killed them, so she agreed. She signed over an inheritance I'd received on the condition that I left there and then. I asked if I could say goodbye to Anthony, but she refused me. She said that as far as Anthony was concerned, I was dead. So, I left. I had no choice."

"Rachel, are you telling me that Lord and Lady Fenwick are your parents? That you...you're Tiffany Fenwick?" Sophie sat forward in shock.

Rachel slowly nodded. "Yes. Yes that is what I am telling you." She pursed her lips, waiting for the reaction from the detective, her lover.

"Fuck."

The silence hung in the air, sucking all the oxygen from the room as each of them took in the magnitude of the situation. Questions floated in and out of Whitton's mind. Some lingered, and others flashed by so fast she had no chance to even consider them.

"Wait, so Anthony?"

"Was just turning eight when I left. He was just a little boy..." Rachel answered.

"And you didn't recognise him, at the pub?"

"No." She shook her head. "I barely even spoke to *Tony.* If I am honest, he creeped me out." More tears escaped at the honest appraisal of her brother. "He was always checking me out." She shuddered and stood, paced the room. "Are you sure?"

"That he is the doll maker?" Sophie clarified. "Pretty sure, yes. We just can't...we don't understand why he is doing it, but as soon as we have DNA, we will have clarification that it is him, yes." She moved towards the door. "I need to fill Dale in."

Rachel continued to pace, the information winding its way around her brain, trying to make sense of it all. When Sophie entered the room again, she asked, "What if...if you had DNA. If it wasn't him, then that would prove it categorically too, right?"

"Yes, of course it would, but if it is him then we will charge him with five murders and one attempted murder," Sophie explained. "We're going to arrest him today, Rachel."

Sophie moved swiftly and took her in her arms. Rachel clung to her like her life depended on it. Her fingers would leave an imprint. "I'll give you my DNA," she whispered.

Chapter Forty-Two

The Duck was quiet as the cars screeched to a halt outside, blue lights flashing and bouncing off of the windows and the snow-covered pavements. All exits were covered as Whitton and Saint walked in through one door. O'Leary and Branson took the other entrance.

Anthony wasn't working, and the girl on shift had no idea where he might be. According to his application form, his last known address was the university he had attended briefly, but that was in a different county. Whitton had requested that local police attend the address anyway and confirm he wasn't there, but she didn't hold out any hope of finding him there.

The DVLA had the same address on record for the car he had owned, the burnt-out remains of which were now sitting in an evidence yard and holding no helpful information.

She left Bowen and Patel to go over the pub, see if there was anything there that he had left that would give clues to his whereabouts or further evidence. Again, she didn't hold out much hope, but Barnard had sent a small group of lab techs along to help anyway. Barnard himself was waiting for the big event.

"Dale, head on over to the big house and see if he is up there." Whitton was annoyed; the worst thing ever was knowing who you wanted and not being able to find them. "I'm going back to the station to talk more to Rachel, see if she can help us unlock something."

~Doll~

The door opened, and Rachel held her breath. The next person to walk through that door would possibly be bringing with them news of her brother's arrest. When it was Sophie who walked in confidently carrying two coffee cups with some files tucked under her arm, she exhaled and felt her shoulders relax a little, until she saw Sophie's face and understood. This was Whitton, the detective. Not Sophie, her lover.

"Rachel, we need to talk about Anthony," she said, taking a seat. "Please, sit with me." She indicated the chair next to her and pulled out her notebook. Only once did she glance at Rachel. She was focused.

"Have you...is he under arrest?" Rachel asked quietly.

"No, that's what I need to talk to you about. I need to question you about Anthony." She fixed eyes with her finally, wanting her to understand that this was her job, it wasn't Sophie and Rachel. "I need to know about your life with your family and I know, I know it will be difficult and uncomfortable, and maybe there are things that under normal circumstances you wouldn't want Sophie to know." Rachel looked up, and Whitton could feel the vulnerability soaking into Rachel as she spoke. "I've two options, Rachel. You can deal with DI Whitton and let me do my job, or I can recuse myself and someone else can ask you these questions."

Rachel's head shook. "I don't want anyone else. I trust you."

"Okay. Tell me about Anthony." She picked up a coffee cup and took a sip.

"I don't...he was just a little boy, and I was a teenager that was fucked up and selfish. I had to leave. I had to," she reiterated. Guilt coursed through her, but she closed her eyes and thought back to that time. "He was a whiney baby, I don't know why, but he would cry a lot, and that would mean my father wouldn't come home, and when he did, he would be drunk..." Whitton pushed the mug of sweet tea towards her. She reached for it and took a sip, wincing at the sweetness. "I don't recall a day when he wasn't drunk. When Anthony was a toddler, he fell down the stairs because my father forgot about him...living in that house was just..." She left it unsaid, but Whitton could imagine.

"What did your mother do?"

"Made excuses for him, covered for him." She rubbed a hand over her face. "I remember one night, we went to a party. He was drunk of course, but insisted on driving home. My mother could have said no, she could drive, but she didn't, and we crashed." She pointed to her torso. "You wanted to know how I got this? My mother told the police that she was driving."

"That's awful."

"Yeah, well they did a lot of awful things. Why do you think I wanted to leave?" She took another sip of the tea, putting the mug down and pushing it away. "Anyway, after that, he was about four at the time...I would wake up to find him in my bed." She smiled sadly at the memory, and then her eyes crinkled and the tears appeared. "First time he was snuggled into my back, I didn't even feel him climb in, but he was there..." She swallowed, and her voice caught in her throat as she tried to continue. "I had...I had this doll, it was my favourite, even though I had grown out of them years ago. I couldn't part with it...he had it in his arms." She wiped her face. "Lots of nights I would wake up after that and find him curled on my bed, sometimes under the covers with me, other times just at the bottom, and always he would be holding the doll, never me, always the doll."

Whitton wrote it all down, word for word. Pulling a photograph from the file, she swiveled it around and showed it to Rachel. It was an image of a chubby-cheeked plastic doll with blonde hair and freckles, with its mouth sewn up in horrifically overexaggerated stitching. "Is this the doll?"

Rachel studied it. She winced at the mouth; the stitching was macabre, but she nodded. "Yes, kind of."

"What's different about it?" Whitton asked, looking at the photograph herself.

"The hair. My doll had dark hair, this has hair like...mine." She could see the minute she had said it that something had clicked in Sophie's mind. Something was whirring inside that clever brain of hers as the cogs turned.

"Silk pajamas?"

"What?" Rachel was confused.

"One of the things we held back from the press. He re-dresses the victims into silk pajamas."

"Oh God." Her eyes closed as the memory hit hard. "I wore silk pajamas, always. My mother insisted on it. 'People like us should dress to impress at all times.'" She air quoted her mother's words.

"It is you. These dolls...in some way they represent you."

"Jesus." Her head dropped in to her hands, fingers scratching at her scalp. "He hates me that much?"

"I don't think it's that," Whitton added, shaking her head. "He's...reverent with them. He cries over them."

"Then why? I don't understand." Whitton had no answer to that just yet. It was the one part of the puzzle that had never made sense, not once they had discovered Gloria Armstrong.

"Okay, let's go back. Your mother, tell me about her."

"My mother..." She looked up at the ceiling as she considered how to reply. "Georgie, that's what we had to call her. Never Mother. She wanted to be my friend, she wanted to hang out. She really couldn't understand that I just wanted a mother."

"She was a party girl, right?" Whitton asked.

"I guess so, they were never at home and when they were, they had all their friends there."

"Drugs?" Rachel nodded. "Sex?" Rachel nodded slowly, her cheeks pinking at the memory.

"Not when we were there, those were the parties that we were sent to Johnathon's." She bit her bottom lip.

"Johnathon?" She watched Rachel's reaction as once again she fought to hold off the tears.

"The man that abused me. My uncle."

"What about Anthony?"

"What about him?" The question confused her.

"Did Johnathon touch Anthony sexually?"

Rachel shook her head rapidly. "No, never, it was only me."

"Are you sure?"

Rachel nodded. "Yes. Positive." She stood up and paced the room. "I was the one he wanted, it was me. Anthony would be asleep."

"Okay." Whitton pulled out the files and was flicking through them when her phone buzzed. She checked the screen and saw Saint's name. "Whitton," she said tersely.

"There isn't anyone here. Apparently the Lord moved out not long after his wife died. It's been bought by some big development company to turn into a hotel."

"Fuck sake." She held the phone against her chest and spoke directly to Rachel. "Your father? He doesn't live at the manor anymore? Do you have any idea where he would be?"

Through her tears, Rachel nodded. "He moved to a nursing home. He isn't well and..." She didn't get to finish.

"Which one?"

Chapter Forty-Three

"He will be so pleased to see you." The nurse spoke jovially as they walked the hall towards his room. Her pristine white uniform rustling with every step annoyed him a little, but he brushed it off. He wasn't here for her. "He hasn't had a visitor for a while." She prattled as they walked, and he did his best to tune her out.

"I know, I have been away, this is the first chance I have had to call in," he managed to reply in time. The corridor was long, everything painted in muted browns and greens. Nauseating. The entire place stank like a canteen mixed with a urinal. He took a certain amount of pleasure knowing this was how his father had ended up.

"It was so lovely when your sister visited, it really cheered him up." She continued talking, and he had kept half an ear on her in case there was anything else a doting son should reply to, but he felt the air leave his lungs at her last comment.

"Sorry, who?"

The nurse stopped and turned to him. "Your sister, she came to see him just after he moved in."

"My...sister?" She was looking at him with concern now. His face was ashen and his breathing had become ragged. The rucksack that he carried fell to the floor with a thud.

"Mr Fenwick, are you okay? Do you need to sit down?" One hand rested on his shoulder, the other on his elbow.

"Yes, yes...I am fine." Picking up the bag, he shrugged it back over his shoulder, "I'm good, let's see the old man."

~Doll~

The police arriving caused a furore amongst the staff and residents of the home. They didn't get excitement like this unless it was on a television screen. DS Saint had exited his vehicle the moment it had come to a halt. Branson, O'Leary, and Bowen all followed as uniformed officers also swarmed the building.

"Lord Fenwick? He staying here?" Saint demanded of the first person in uniform that passed them.

"Y-yes," she stammered. "He, uh. Sorry, what do you want?"

"I'm DS Saint, my colleagues and I need to speak to Lord Fenwick urgently." He spoke with confidence. His left hand held his warrant card, his team automatically holding theirs out for inspection too.

"I'll have to find Mrs Hunter."

"No, you need to tell me which room is Lord Fenwick's, now," he insisted. They didn't have time to wait around for whoever Mrs Hunter was. "Show me," he demanded, gently guiding her by the elbow. She seemed to consider something before finally turning and telling them to follow her.

She walked quickly, used to traipsing back and forth through these corridors all day long. Dale noted how clean and neat-looking it was. Everything was freshly painted in calming greens and browns. He imagined life here would be quite comfortable for the likes of Lord Fenwick.

"He is just in here," she said, knocking lightly on the door. Number 43 in gold lettering was painted perfectly on a white background. O'Leary moved her aside. Wrapping her bony hand around the door lever, she pushed down, opening the door wide for them all to enter.

The room was moderately decorated. Lord Fenwick's room had a lived-in feel. His clothes were strewn haphazardly, hanging from chairs and the unslept on side of the bed. He had a few photographs, all of which showed him in his youth, out on the town with Georgina by his side, but no Lord Fenwick.

"Where else could he be?" Branson said. Bowen and Saint moved around the room. Andy Bowen pulled out a drawer and sucked in a breath.

"Guv, look at this." He held the object in between gloved fingertips: a doll.

"I guess he could be in the lounge, or out in the gardens maybe. He doesn't often go out there, but with his son visiting then he-" The nurse stopped speaking, glancing nervously between the two detectives. They looked horrified.

"What? His son? Tall guy, shaved head?" Saint was bending down, examining a spot of reddish brown on the carpet. He had an empty picture frame in his hand, which had clearly held a photograph. Acknowledging the doll with a nod of his head, he turned his attention to the nurse again.

"Yes, that's him."

Saint moved to the door, followed by Branson. "What was in this frame?"

"His daughter's picture, I think."

"Andy, stay here and get S.O.C.O in and check that stain." With that, he turned to the nurse. "Which way?"

Chapter Forty-Four

Lord Fenwick was nowhere to be found. Every available officer had helped search the grounds, and nothing. He had literally just disappeared. Nobody had seen him or his visitor.

Jeff Branson once again found himself sitting in front of TV screens reviewing CCTV. Communal areas and the outside were all under surveillance. Anthony had arrived just 40 minutes before they had. He had pulled up in a car, climbed out of the passenger side, and then strolled in.

"Dale," Jeff called out. The DS poked his head around the door. "Get a search going on this plate." He held out his arm and stretched to reach Saint, passing a piece of paper with the car registration number scribbled on it. "No doubt it's a cab, but it could be a friend."

"On it."

Branson went back to viewing the tapes. He watched as Anthony entered into the main reception area and spoke to the same nurse they had dealt with earlier. They spoke for a couple of minutes before he signed in and followed her down the corridor. "Dale!" he shouted again. Once more, the blonde head of Saint poked back around the door.

"Yes, what ya got?"

"Downstairs, he signed in." Dale nodded and was gone in a shot.

~Doll~

Woodington Police Station was eerily quiet in the office. It was all hands on deck at the nursing home, and Whitton was feeling the pressure. She wanted to be out there, channeling the investigation.

She had gone over and over and over everything that Rachel could possibly remember about her family and its fucked-up relationships. But in the end, she had to admit that she didn't think there was much else she could tell her until they spoke to Anthony or her father.

With Rachel's shift due to start at 2 p.m., Whitton had agreed that she could go. Then Sophie had questioned whether or not it was a good idea.

"What else am I going to do?" Rachel had said. Sophie sat perched on the edge of the desk with Rachel nestled between her thighs. "I'm better off staying busy and being around people until this is all over."

Breathing deeply, Sophie exhaled slowly and let her palms rub lightly up and down Rachel's spine. "I know, I just don't like it that we haven't got him yet."

"I'll be fine, its not like he knows I am his sister." Her hands rose up from where they had rested on Sophie's chest and cupped her cheeks. She leant in and placed a soft kiss on her lips. "I'll be at work, surrounded by people, and I won't go home until you call, okay?"

Reluctantly, Sophie nodded. Kissing Rachel's forehead, she let her hands drop to the desk, her eyes following Rachel as she walked away.

"Sophie?" She had reached the door, but turned back. "Is my father okay?"

"Honestly, I don't know. Anthony has been there though."

Rachel nodded. "I went to see him...my father, when I first got back...he isn't a bad person, just ill, ya know? The drink, it's got its claws into him." She smiled sadly, hearing herself make excuses for him, just like her mother had.

"I'll let you know as soon as I know anything, okay?"

~Doll~

With Rachel gone, Sophie waited. Standing outside, she took the opportunity to have a break. She pulled the cigarettes from her pocket and lit one. Her phone had buzzed, a text message from Yvonne, checking she was okay and informing her that she had had the flat valued and would be making an offer to buy her out. It felt like months had passed since they had split. Christmas was literally just around the corner, and she hadn't even thought about it. Wrapping up this case would be the best Christmas present she could think of.

She wrote out a quick message back, letting her know that she was fine, and they would talk about the flat in the new year.

Wishing her a merry Christmas, she pressed send and pocketed the phone. Her mind already back on the job.

Jogged from her thoughts by the buzzing of her phone as it rang again from inside her pocket, she flicked the remnants of the cigarette out into the road and grabbed the vibrating device.

"Whitton."

"It's me," Dale Saint said. "We've got a doll but no body."

"Alright, I'll head over and-"

"Wait, Soph...Rachel, I think he might know about her." She felt the air rush out of her lungs. "I mean, look, the father had a photograph of her and it's not in the frame."

"Okay. Fuck. Alright, leave the team on it your end, I'm going to check on Rachel. I want you back here to go through everything we have so far."

~Doll~

With Rachel assuring her that she was safe, Sophie found Dale waiting for her in the conference room. He looked up as she came through the door, a tight smile adorning his face.

"Rachel confirmed, she gave her father a photograph; it was a goodbye present. All that he asked of her." She plonked the files she carried down on the desk. "Right, lay it out for me."

"Okay, well Lord Fenwick moved into what can only be described as a nursing home."

"He seems a bit young," Sophie interrupted.

"Basically, he has onset Parkinson's and several alcohol-related issues, and his name held sway. He moved in about a month after his wife died, apparently he didn't like living by himself." He held his notepad in his left hand and used the finger on his right to scan down the page. "Not long after he moved in, Rachel visited. After that, the staff said he seemed to smile a little more, and the photograph appeared. That same photograph is now missing. The frame was smashed, and we found blood on the carpet in Lord Fenwick's room."

Sophie ran her fingers through her hair. "Fresh?"

He nodded. "Yep, it was still wet."

"Shit, okay, so we've got a missing Lord Fenwick. Where would he take him? And how did they get there?" She stood now, pacing as she tried to think.

"Jeff has him arriving in a cab, but there isn't anything on camera showing them leaving, so we have to assume they made their way across the field at the back that would lead them into Branford."

"Where he can easily call another cab?"

"Yes, and O'Leary was on it, she found a cab firm that did pick up two people that bore that description and dropped them at a doctor's surgery on Rumpole Street."

"Ok, good, so we have a rough area to work with." She walked across to the board and looked at the map, searching with her finger for Rumpole Street. "What else?" she asked, her back to him as she continued to search.

"He signed in as...The Doll Maker." Her head turned slowly, the rest of her following until she faced him. He was nodding at her. "Yep, the fucking doll maker, can you believe that?"

"It's his end game. This is it, everything he did comes to an end now, with the father." She turned back to the board and banged her finger against the map. "Myrtle Street, it's four streets away from the doctor's surgery."

Chapter Forty-Five

Nicholas Fenwick's head hurt. He felt woozy, which wasn't a strange feeling per se, but this was a little different. Usually he felt numb; this time it was painful. He was finding it difficult to get his thoughts straight. His eyesight came in and out of focus. Looking around the room, he could see that he wasn't at the home anymore. He had never been anywhere that looked like this, and the stench – what was that god-awful smell?

"Daddy, nice of you to join me." Sarcasm dripped off his tongue as Anthony sat crossed-legged on the floor, just like he did when he was a little boy. "What do you think of my place? Yeah, it's not looking its best right now, but that's because the police had to rip it apart when they found Mummy." He could see his father struggling to comprehend what he was talking about. "Oh, I know, she wasn't *really* Mummy, or should I say, Georgie." He cackled with laughter and in an instant, he was on his feet, his face pushed up close to his father's. "That bitch went and died all by herself. I needed a replacement, did you read about it? It was all over the news." He jumped from joist to joist. The floorboards from underneath, where he had placed Gloria's body, had been ripped up by forensics, leaving gaping holes between the beams.

"Did you like the doll I made for you?"

"Anthony, pack it in." He spoke slowly, his voice slurred, and for once it wasn't from the drink. He heard his son laughing again.

"Pack it in," he mocked. Creeping up behind his father, he grasped his hair and yanked his head back so he could stare into his face. "Or what, will you send me to my room? Send me away again? Get rid of me so you can fuck your bimbos and drink yourself into oblivion while your children...while your daughter kills herself?" Reaching into his pocket, he pulled out a cut-throat razor and unfolded it. Light from the lamp glinted off the hilt. "That's what she did, right? That's what you told me." He placed the flat side of the blade against his father's throat. "When I wanted to see her, what was it you said?" The knife slowly twisted until it glided lightly across the skin, cutting through the epidermis in a thin red line. His father struggled against the binds that held him in place on the chair, his Adam's apple gulping. "Now, now Papa, you don't want to miss all the fun, do you?" He came around the chair and stood in front of him, bending at the waist as he drew the knife down his father's cheek. "What was it you said?"

"Anthony, stop this." He tried again to appeal to his son, his voice cracking with fear, where it had once been stern and confident with the boy.

"Don't tell me what to do!" he screamed, his face contorted with rage. "What did you say?!"

Nicholas Fenwick tried to get his mind together, to find the words Anthony wanted to hear. "I said...that...it wasn't something you should...see." Anthony punched him in the face. His head whipped back and forth, his brain turning more to mush.

"That isn't what you said, Daddy. What did you say?" he hissed at him. "Shall I tell you?" Another cut down the other cheek, this time cutting deeper into the dermis. Ignoring his father's scream's, he continued. "You said, and I quote, 'she's already gone, you didn't need to see that *bloody* mess, boy.'"

"You...idi-idiot..." Fenwick senior's laughter turning to a choking cough. When he finally caught his breath, Anthony punched him again, once, twice, and then a third time. The world went black for Nicholas Fenwick, which was probably a good thing for him as Anthony brought the razor to his arm and went to work.

~Doll~

"Wakey, wakey, Daddy." His mocking tones drifted in and out of Lord Fenwick's hearing. His eyes flickered open, and with that came the unbearable pain of a hundred cuts inflicted upon the flesh of his arms. He wanted to scream, but his jaw hurt from the numerous punches Anthony had thrown. Any remnant of alcohol in his system had long since lost its ability to numb his nerves.

"Anthony, please...you don't have to do this," he mumbled around the bruising. He felt like he had been to the dentist, his lips fat and sore.

"Oh, but I do...you see, I have spent almost my entire life believing a lie, haven't I?" He was sitting again, legs crossed, wiping the knife on his shirt. "The only thing in the world that I had was her, my sister." He was calmer now, and Fenwick figured maybe he stood a chance to get out of here. "She killed herself because you and mother just couldn't stop." His fingers rubbed around his chin as he looked at his handywork. The razor lay abandoned on the floor. "But you lied, didn't you?"

Fenwick shook his head. "No..." He was so tired, so very tired. "I never lied-"

"You lied!!" Anthony shouted. "I didn't need to see the bloody mess!!! I was eight, and you let me think my sister killed herself, and then, as if that wasn't bad enough...when all I needed were my parents to hold me and tell me it would all be okay...you packed me off to boarding school."

"It wasn't like that..."

"Did you even care?" Anthony asked him. His head tilted, and for a moment he reminded Nicholas of the little boy he once was.

"Of course, we- "

"Don't play with me." He grabbed a knife from the bag and without pause, plunged it into his father's shoulder. "Every day of my life, bullied and beaten all because you wanted to party and drink, fucking your bimbos while mother watched, or was it more fun watching mother get shafted by all your friends?" He twisted his fist and turned the knife. "Scream, go on... nobody is coming to save you."

Chapter Forty-Six

They were ready, stab vests on. The car slowed to a halt, the tyre bouncing gently against the kerb. It was getting darker, winter nights drawing in early. They could see the house from the car. The windows were boarded up. 'Do not cross' tape hung across the front of the gate and fencing.

"OK, if he is in there, then he has the upper hand already," Whitton said, twisting in her seat to speak to all occupants of the car. Branson and Bowen had climbed in from their own vehicle that was now parked behind. "Andy, you stay at the front. It looks like it's still sealed as forensics left it, but that doesn't mean he won't use it to make a run for it. Jeff, Dale, you both come in with me." Her eyes were focused and ready. "It's my guess, if he is using this place, then he has to be sneaking in via the back door. So, it's the kitchen at the back, that leads out into the hall, and from there it's the dining room on the right. Front of the house is the living room."

With the street lamp to guide them, they crept up to the house and along the path that led to the front door. Bowen took up position whilst the other three moved silently to the right-side of the semi-detached building, a small alley leading around the house to the back. Branson led, his torch pointing downwards to the floor. Branches from next door's bushes poked at them as they brushed past.

The board that had covered the back entrance now only leaned against it. It had clearly been jimmied. Gently, Sophie and

Jeff took a side each and moved it to the side. With Dale now holding the torch, they followed him in.

The kitchen was empty. Every cupboard had been emptied. Some had been pulled apart, doors taken off. Linoleum that had been on the floor was gone; just a concrete base was left, bare and empty, like the lives that had been lived here.

With a sweep of the torch, the three of them moved through and into the hall. In single file they moved slowly, listening for any sign that they were not alone.

Saint stopped abruptly and held his hand up.

"Did you hear that?" he whispered over his shoulder. They stood still and listened. There was a low moan, barely audible. Whitton nodded, and they moved forward again. The door to the dining room was shut. Whitton reached out and slowly turned the handle. She winced when the hinges creaked as the door opened. Jeff moved past her and walked inside the room. Empty.

Shaking his head, he slipped back into the hall and they all turned as one towards the living room; the same room Gloria Armstrong's body had been found in.

~Doll~

Nicholas Fenwick was rushed by ambulance to Woodington University Hospital. Sophie had left with Dale as soon as she saw it: Rachel's photograph held in place by a knife stabbed into the chest of their father.

She raced through the traffic as best she could, screeching to a halt outside of the hospital, leaving Dale to chase behind.

"Rachel Carter, I need to speak to her right now!" she practically bellowed at the first nurse she came across. Theatres were closed off to members of the public; only staff with a pass and the code could get in there.

"I think she is in Theatre Two," the nurse mumbled, shaken by the demand. "They're dealing with a heart attack."

"*Thinking* isn't good enough, I need to know. Is she in there or not?" Sophie grabbed ahold of the nurse by her arms.

"Guv," a gentle cough came from behind her as Dale caught up. She shook herself and realised how she looked right now.

"Sorry." She dropped her hands and let go of the nurse, who took the chance to scuttle off, looking back just the once before doubling her efforts and disappearing around the corner.

"You ok?" Dale asked.

Exhaling, Sophie nodded. "Yeah, she's in theatre."

"Ok, that's good." He looked around. "Why don't you grab a seat and I'll go get us some coffee. The ambulance will be here any minute."

"Yeah, okay, thanks Dale." Feeling a little perturbed, she flopped into one of the uncomfortable plastic seats and dropped her head into her hands. She wasn't used to this. What made her a good detective was her ability to remain remote and keep her emotions in check. Her need for justice had been the only emotional connection she ever felt to a case and the people involved in it. She was pretty sure she should probably remove herself from the case altogether, but she was in too deep now.

There was a commotion to her right as Nicholas Fenwick was wheeled along the corridor. Medical staff on either side of the bed moved along quickly with him, discussing his injuries over the top of him. Medical jargon and terminology that Whitton didn't quite understand was thrown back and forth between the medics.

Whitton stood and followed behind. "Is he going to make it?"

A short man in scrubs at the back of the gurney turned to her. "Dunno, he's in a bad way. Multiple stab wounds." Whitton nodded, following along. The doors to theatre opened and she kept walking, hoping nobody would notice. At the last minute, the same guy turned and shook his head. "No further, please."

"Okay." She held both palms up. "I need to speak to Rachel Carter."

"I'll see what I can do," he called back over his shoulder as the bed and Nicholas Fenwick moved out of sight.

~Doll~

"You gonna be like that all day?" Saint asked, looking up from his phone. He was playing a game of Scrabble, and Whitton's pacing back and forth was distracting. She stopped moving and glared at him. "Do you want me to try and get hold of Becky?"

Whitton sat down opposite him and began to gnaw on a thumbnail. "Yes, but that would be inappropriate."

"Yeah, probably, but murdering you would be a little more inappropriate, and that's on the cards if you don't calm the fuck down." He grinned at her and earned himself another glare. She sighed and slumped down further into the chair.

"I dunno what's wrong with me."

"Welcome to the world of emotions." He laughed, becoming serious again in an instant. "Look, you like her, maybe even more than that, and now..." He shrugged. "You're just as human as the rest of us. If this was Becky, I'd be going out of my mind too."

"I'm not..." She stood up and began pacing again. "I do like her, but that's not...you're right, I'm off the ball on this...I know Becky jokes about my surly nature, but she's right. Nothing puts me off my game, and yet..." She raked her fingers through her hair. "She's under my skin...if anything happens to her, I'm not sure I can..." she was interrupted from her thoughts by a doctor, still in scrubs and covered in blood.

"Detectives, Lord Fenwick didn't make it." He spoke solemnly, as though they knew the man personally. Whitton imagined he had a good bedside manner.

"Right," Whitton said, moving from one foot to the other. "I need to speak with Rachel Carter urgently."

"Ah yes, I did ask, and apparently her brother came to collect her."

~Doll~

All hell broke loose as Saint took charge. Speaking into his phone, he passed the information on to Branson. Grabbing hold of Whitton's arm, he tugged her along with him.

"Right, get the fuck over it." He leant into her and spoke quietly. "If we're going to save her then I need Whitton here, not Sophie. So, put a fucking block on it, do whatever it is you used to do, and start thinking. Where would he take her?"

Whitton gulped in air and pushed every single feeling she had deep down. "I need a minute," she hissed, pulling herself free from his grip. The women's toilet was just there, and she pushed the door open, slamming it into the wall. The woman at the mirror, washing her hands, jumped. Within seconds she was alone. She paced the small space, dragging her fingers through her hair, growling in frustration, her palms flat against the basin. She stared up at herself in the mirror. She looked a mess. Her hair needed washing and hung lankly down the side of her face. Reaching a hand up, she tucked it behind her ear.

"Okay, get it together." She nodded at herself in the mirror and ran the tap, splashing her face with ice cold water. "She needs you to pull it together."

Chapter Forty-Seven

Rachel knew it was a mistake the moment she stepped foot outside. The intention to just have a sneaky cigarette had become the catalyst to something much bigger. She kicked herself now, her naïveté in thinking that nothing could happen to her, that she was safe here at work. She truly believed that Anthony would not come here looking for her. It was foolish to surmise, but the risk she had taken had now come full circle.

Anthony was all grown up, a strapping six-foot-something man with broad shoulders and a grip that made a vice look weak. He was wearing the uniform of an orderly, fitting in perfectly as he strolled the corridors searching her out. Following a group of nurses, he easily slipped inside the doors that led down to theatres. They hadn't even questioned him. He had an air of confidence about him, a belief that he was invincible.

He found her within minutes – a few questions here and there, everybody so very helpful. He explained he was her brother and that she was needed in a family emergency. Of course, they had pointed him in the right direction immediately. All he had to do now was wait until she was alone.

He couldn't believe his luck when she wandered off by herself towards an exit door, sliding her hand inside her pocket and pulling out a packet of cigarettes. He grimaced at that. Smoking, such a nasty habit. Then he laughed to himself sardonically as he realised it was no different to his joints, and soon enough, it wouldn't matter. She was going to die anyway.

~Doll~

Now, Rachel was sitting in her own living room with her brother quietly wandering around the space, picking up ornaments and pieces of her life, questioning her about where each trinket came from.

"What about this?" he asked, holding a small colourful plate that clearly had Tenerife painted on it.

She was hopeful. The longer this went on for, the more chance she had that Sophie would come for her, and this time she didn't care if they smashed the door in; she needed her lover to save her.

"Tenerife," she answered as calmly as she could muster. His intense gaze fell on her. He had blue eyes like their father, red hair like their mother, though he had shaved it all off. It suited him like that, she thought. She was the opposite: green eyes like her mother, and blonde like their father.

He didn't look like a killer; he looked like her brother. Not how she thought he would grow up to be, but she could see the similarities in their faces. The same nose and shape of their chins. He was handsome, in a way.

"And this?" he asked, holding another piece of pottery in the form of a small jug.

"Wales...Anthony, can we talk?" She had to try and find common ground with him. There had to be some way in which she could talk her way out of this. They were family, after all.

"About what?" he asked, nonplussed as he continued to peruse the shelves of knick-knacks and bric-a-brac. A life lived without his presence.

The question dumbfounded her for a second. What did he think she wanted to talk about? "Maybe we can start with-"

"Hmm, I know..." He suddenly swung around to face her. "Let's start with why you fucking left me?" he bellowed at her, his face now red and angry.

"Okay, we...we can start there." She wanted to move, to find a more comfortable position, but she daren't. "I had no choice-"

"Choice? *Choice?*" he screamed. "What choice did I have?" He moved so fast across the room that he was upon her in an instant, bending into her and forcing her backwards into the back of the sofa with a slap to her cheek. He was huge and menacing, and she felt the prick of tears at the sting of his palm.

"I tried so very hard to stay," she stuttered, and she had, that was the truth of it. But, Johnathon had made it impossible, and their parents didn't care. "I wanted to stay, I wanted-" His hand raised again, coming down with the force he intended.

"No, you escaped, and you left me behind." He sniffed, fighting the urge to cry. He wouldn't cry over it again. Not after all he had done, telling their story. And it had all been a lie.

"Anthony, I didn't..." She tried to think of the words that might appease him, "Mother told me-" He put his hands over his ears.

"I don't want to hear about her," he said, shaking his head furiously back and forth. He looked like a petulant child.

"Then how can I explain?" she asked gently. He didn't move, didn't speak. She sighed and tried again. "Johnathon, Uncle Johnny. Remember him? Staying at his house?" He looked at her then. Slowly he nodded, not taking his eyes off her. She gulped and tried to steady herself. "You remember how we were sent there, when they wanted to party?" Again, he nodded. "When you went to bed...Uncle Johnny would...he would behave very badly. From when you were very little, just a baby and I was...just a child."

"What did he do?"

She hadn't talked about this in detail for a very long time. There had been no need to until now; it was dealt with. "When he was alone with me...he would, do things...things that uncles shouldn't do with children. Even before you were born."

His eyes narrowed at her as he understood where this was heading. His face grew redder and she prepared herself for the inevitable slap, but it didn't come. Instead, he moved away and went back to perusing her shelves.

"Is that why you're a dyke?" he asked, turning to face her as he fondled a china windmill from Amsterdam.

"No, of course not." She felt her own anger begin to build. "Don't you dare judge me." She swallowed nervously as she watched him. He laughed.

"Oh, dear sister, I am not judging you, quite frankly I'd fuck her too. She's hot in a 'fuck off and leave me alone' kind of way. I'd love nothing more than to bend her over and give it to her." He smirked at her. "I doubt though that she will want you once she finds out who you are."

"Who am I? You don't know me, or anything about me!" She glared at him. If she was going to die then so be it; she wouldn't go down whimpering like a victim though. She stood and moved towards him. He hadn't anticipated that, and he flinched slightly. "And you don't know *anything* about her either."

"Maybe you're right, but then maybe I'll leave you just like I left the others." He grinned and produced the knife from his pocket and flicked it open. "At least I don't have to remove the spleen this time," he cackled.

"What happened to you?" she asked him. He seemed to falter at that, stumbling over a mental image of himself as a small boy.

"Why do you care?" he asked, turning the knife over in his palm as he stared at it rather than her.

"Of course I care, Anthony. You might have done some awful things, but...you are still my brother." She reached out a tentative hand and gently laid her fingertips against his arm. His eyes followed the movement and stared at her fingers until she removed them.

"You're the first person to ask me that," he said. His eyes closed as he considered something. "Uncle Johnny was your monster. Mine was Robert Barrington-West." He shuddered even speaking his name.

"I don't know who he is." Rachel spoke quietly, unwilling to disrupt him.

"Why would you, Tiffany?" Hearing herself being called by her name for the first time in years felt surreal; for a moment it didn't even register that he was speaking to her. She even glanced to the door to see if someone else had entered the room.

"I haven't been Tiffany in a very long time."

"You'll always be Tiffany to me." His hand moved, and reflexively she flinched backwards, expecting the harsh slap against her skin, but he didn't hit her. Instead, he stroked the back of his fingers down her cheek. "I'm sorry I hit you. I just get so very angry sometimes."

"It's okay," she lied. "Tell me about Robert." Just the mention of his name turned Anthony's face into a contortion of anger and sadness.

"He was a bully. A nasty cretin that made my life a living hell," he spat.

Chapter Forty-Eight

The drive back to the station from the hospital was slow and torturous. Weaving in and out of the traffic, Dale had done his best to avoid the busier roads. Whitton was silent, focused solely on where he would take her.

They had scoured the hospital. Every available officer had been given the task of searching each and every room, cupboard, and floor. And they found nothing. CCTV had shown what looked like a nurse and a man walking closely together towards the car park, but then they had lost them.

Colleen O'Leary was once again calling around cab companies, trying to find out if anyone had picked them up, and was not having much luck.

"It's a good job this isn't America and we don't have guns," Saint said quietly to Jeff as they poured coffee together. "God knows what Whitton would do if she caught him now."

"So, is she and this Rachel...they doing it?"

Dale looked around before speaking. "Not my place to say, but suffice to say this one's more than personal now."

"Got it." Jeff nodded. "Mum's the word then," he added, tapping the side of his nose. Dale nodded and turned away, carrying coffees for himself and Whitton.

As he reached the desk, she stood, grabbing her phone and pulling her vest from the back of the chair. "He has to have taken her to her place," she said. The urgency in her voice told him that this wasn't up for debate. "I've gone through everything, and other than the big house, which is now a building site, it has to be her place."

"Okay, so let's go." He put the mugs down on the desk and began to put his own vest on, stopping in his tracks when he felt her palm on his bicep.

"If you want to sit this out..." She breathed deeply. "I don't...look, just don't put your career on the line for me, okay?"

"I won't," he said. "Cos I'm not going to let you do anything stupid, alright?" She nodded, a tight grin appearing on her lips. This was her partner; they had each other's backs, and that was all that mattered.

"Okay, let's go," she said, slapping him on the shoulder. "Jeff, Andy, Colleen...you coming?" She moved quickly to the door, listening to the onslaught of questions that came from them all inquiring where they were going.

~Doll~

Anthony had told her a tale of a lonely little boy who had been packed off to boarding school and forgotten about. He only came home for holidays because the school didn't entertain keeping children for the duration. A nanny had been employed for those weeks, and although she was a spiteful bitch who had no patience and certainly no love inside her, it was a respite from the hell he suffered at Farlington Hall Academy.

Robert Barrington-West was, in real terms, a nasty little sadist who enjoyed nothing more than inflicting pain, emotionally or physically, and he had picked out Anthony Fenwick as his target. From day one, Anthony would be cornered and given a quick beating. Kicks and punches flew rapidly as the small eight-year-old tried valiantly to defend himself against the older, bigger boy's onslaught. When beating him was no longer so much fun, he began locking him in a trunk. For hours young Anthony would be on his knees, bent over and tucked in as the lid was closed down on him. His legs and arms would go numb, and the pain would be excruciating. Often he would pass out with the lack of oxygen. Now and then Robert would kick the trunk, or worse still, tumble it over, rolling it around the room to cackles of laughter from his gang of terrified pals – none of which were confident that they wouldn't end up suffering the same treatment if they so much as dared to go against anything that Robert came up with.

As Anthony got older, the punishments took on a more sadistic nature. He would beg to go home. The few times his parents called, or were at home during the holidays, he would plead with them not to send him back. But his pleas fell on deaf ears. Nobody was going to speak up for him. They all refused to see it.

When Robert turned sixteen and Anthony was just twelve, he became fixated with stripping the boy and having him perform for him. Some days it would simply be to stand naked at the window on a freezing winter's day. On other occasions he would bend him over the bed and sodomise him with an implement, before finally succumbing to his urges and using his penis.

When Anthony cried the first time, Robert had simply run a bath and held his head under water until he passed out. Anthony didn't cry the next time.

"I'm so-"

"Don't say you're fucking sorry, Tiffany," he growled, his eyes brimming with unshed tears. Hers were overflowing. In all the years since she had left home, not once had she ever considered that life for Anthony would be like this.

"But, I am...Jesus, Anthony."

"What? You were dead, what could you possibly have done for me?" he snapped back.

"What do you mean? I wasn't dead, I'm not dead, Anthony." The tears he had been holding back now tumbled over long lashes and slid down the side of his nose.

"I fucking know that now, don't I?" he shouted. Grabbing her by her shoulders, he shook her. "You've ruined everything. Now, my work is worthless!" As he let go of her, he pushed her to the floor. "All of this..." He swept the room with his arm. "Everything was for you! All of it...a legacy, and now...you're alive, and everything I have worked for is worthless."

"What do you mean? Tell me, I don't understand."

He dropped to the floor and sat himself in front of her, crossing his legs like a little boy. He rocked back and forth as he stared at her.

"You, they said you killed yourself." She gasped, and went to speak, but he placed a finger to his own lips, indicating she be quiet. "Father said, you were a bloody mess and that was why I couldn't see you. Then they sent me to school and you were never mentioned again."

"But-"

"Shut up," he spat, still rocking. "I didn't plan any of this. All of it was just...she wouldn't stop talking." His hands went to his ears. Rachel was confused. "I had to kill her. I mean, I just knew...it was like an epiphany." He laughed then and said, "An epiphany for Tiffany. I did it all for you, in your memory, picked those that I thought would look like you." He tilted his head to look at her. "I thought you'd be smaller."

"Who did you have to kill?"

"Mother! Who else?" He looked at her as though she were stupid. "Of course, the bitch had to ruin that for me by fucking dying all by herself."

"Anthony, you're not making any sense." Her words were barely out before he leant forward, nose-to-nose, and glared at her.

"Just listen!" He cocked an ear as though there was something to be heard. "Do you hear that?"

She shook her head and winced as she realised that her eye and lip were now beginning to bruise. He closed his eyes and started to rock sideways instead. It was strangely hypnotic, and easily the most terrifying image she had ever witnessed.

"They want me to kill you too," he whispered. "But, I won't, and now they're mad with me."

"Who...who w-wants you to do that?" Her eyes widened in fear.

"My friends, the ones that help me choose." He smiled at her and reached his hands out, taking hers within his own. "But, I said no." He grinned again. "Not yet."

She needed a plan. Looking at the clock on the mantle, she could see that they had been here for over an hour. Every minute that passed seemed to take her hope further away. Sophie wasn't coming, and her brother was becoming increasingly more fractured.

"Gloria was a whore. I used to pay her to let me do all the things Robert forced me to do." He looked to the ceiling and grinned. "She was a filthy, vile and disgusting human being, but needs must. I read the newspaper headline, did you see it? Mother was dead...at first, I was happy, and then I became angry...I realised I had wanted to kill her. My *friends* told me it would be ok, if I killed Gloria instead, then I would feel happier...they were right." His thoughts seemed to jump just as easily as he did. He jumped up and threw himself onto the sofa, stretching out, he yawned. His eyes closed and his breathing slowed. Rachel's heart raced as she considered the thought that he might just fall asleep and she could take her chance.

She waited, and waited. It felt like an eternity before she heard it: a light snoring. Holding her breath, she moved slowly, kneeling at first before pushing herself upwards to stand. "Where are you going?" His voice sounded louder in the silence. He was sitting up, and she hadn't even heard him move.

"I was...I need a drink," she stammered, pointing towards the kitchen.

"No, you were going to leave me again, weren't you?" His head tilted and he looked at her quizzically. "Don't you like me, Tiffany?"

"Of course I do, I'm just thirsty...Don't you want a drink?"

He shook his head. "No, I think maybe I might kill you now though."

Epilogue

Spring had sprung. The bulbs had begun to bloom and push their way into the world. Blossoms clung to the trees, covering the shy branches, colouring the greyness, and bringing with it a brightness that had been lacking these past months.

The snow had melted away, and with it had gone the coldness that had held Woodington in its clutches for so long.

Whitton lifted another box and carried it inside, passing Dale as he returned empty-handed to grab the next one. Moving through the door, she took the stairs one at a time.

The room was neat. Her new double bed with its fresh sheets and new bedding was immaculate, but it wouldn't be for long. She grinned at the thought of messing it up. This room, this house, it was a new start. Somewhere she could call her own and put her stamp on it.

"Hey, you just gonna stand around or actually help with these other boxes?" Becky said. She placed the box she was carrying down alongside the others.

"Yes, I am coming. Just... looking around the place."

Becky nudged her shoulder with her own. "It's a great place. You're gonna be happy here ya know, things will...you know."

Sophie nodded and put the box she was carrying down next to the others.

Yvonne had made an offer on the flat, and Sophie had accepted without thought or argument. Her ex-girlfriend was happy and about to attempt her first IVF treatment. Sophie had wished her all the best and promised to keep in touch, but something in the back of her mind told her that she wouldn't. It was time to move forwards.

Everyone was moving forward and that was what she needed to do too, so she used most of the money to put a deposit down on this place, and she spent what was left on new furniture and getting the place redecorated. It was home.

She had taken a month off work straight after the Doll Maker wrapped up. Doctor's orders. Anthony Fenwick had taken his own life, so there would be no trial. His victims would get no justice, and for that Whitton was sorry, but she wouldn't ever be sorry that he was dead. He didn't deserve to live after everything he had done.

They had found the lock-up where he had holed up, filled with an acrid stench of marijuana and burning plastic. The place looked like a plastic slaughterhouse – broken body parts from unused dolls strewn everywhere. He had clearly taken his time to get them just right. Those that didn't work or that he had made mistakes with were ripped apart and strewn around the space. They found the missing body parts from the victims too, stashed inside the body of a larger Doll that took pride of place in his makeshift bed. Joint butts scattered the floor – hundreds of tiny white, rolled tobacco papers stuffed with weed. It was an awful, macabre space, and she was glad to see the back of it.

Taking the stairs down, two at a time, she reached the van and passed Dale again as he wandered back in with another box. She thought about him for a minute. Until now, she had never had anyone she would label a best friend. Her entire life she had been a bit of a loner, making her way through life without really caring about whether there was anyone else in it with her. But now, she had Dale and Becky, and the kids. She loved those kids, and at least once a week she babysat while Becky and Dale enjoyed date night. Becky had told her she was a godsend, but she believed that they were sent for her. This family that had adopted her into it had been just what she needed.

Since that night when the Doll Maker had finally accomplished everything he had set out to do, Dale had been there by her side. It was he who had driven them to the house. He was the one who found the lifeless form of Rachel laid out on her couch as though she were sleeping, and it was he who dealt with Sophie when she broke down. When her legs gave way, and she was falling to the floor, it was Dale Saint who caught her. He got her out of there and away from prying eyes, bundled her up into the back of the ambulance and stayed with her the entire time.

He organised his colleagues and liaised with Dr Barnard and his staff. Dale Saint was a rock when she needed him most, and she would forever remember that.

There were plenty of dark days. Those first few in the immediate aftermath had shaken Whitton to the core. She spent a week at the hospital, refusing to leave, not that they were going to kick her out, and it was Dale and Becky who made sure she ate something, brought her fresh clothes and forced her to shower.

It had been three months, and only now was she truly able to breathe easily and enjoy some inner peace. She woke each morning feeling thankful.

Looking up into the back of the van, she laid eyes on her: the woman she had gone through all of this for. The woman she now knew she would go through anything for.

"Hey, ready for another one?" Rachel asked, smiling down at her, green eyes sparkling as she waited for a reply. Sophie heaved herself up into the back of the van.

"Actually, I was ready for something else." She grinned and moved in closer, enjoying the scent of her that filled the small van. She couldn't take her eyes from her. When they had first entered the house and Rachel was just lying there, it had almost killed Sophie. It was in that moment that she realised her feelings had evolved, she was in love with her, and she had failed her. She hadn't been smart enough, quick enough. The world still moved around her in a blur. She could see Dale checking for a pulse, heard him shouting for an ambulance, but it hadn't registered right away. Rachel was alive – barely.

"Oh, and what would that be?" Rachel asked, allowing Sophie's arms to wrap around her torso and tug her closer. Since that night, when Anthony had wrapped his hands around her neck and squeezed until he thought the life had left her, she had yearned for Sophie's touch. Her last cognisant thoughts had been of the brooding and surly detective, silently praying even in those last moments that she would save her.

When she awoke in the hospital and found the tousled hair of her lover within reach of her fingertips, it had taken all her strength not to cry out and wake her.

She had found out later that Anthony had killed their father, and then, believing he had killed her also, he had killed himself. It had taken a while to get through that, but Sophie had been there the entire time, loving her in a way only Sophie could.

"This..." Sophie said, brushing their lips together, tenderly cradling her chin before a small voice perked up. Their lips curled into a smile as they both stared down at the wispy-haired blonde kid with blue eyes staring up at them in disgust.

"Eww. Auntie Sophie, stop kissing Rachel, you'll get germs!" Ella grimaced at them before returning to the task in hand, pushing a large box to the edge for someone to take.

"What's germs?" asked Harry as she tugged on Sophie's leg.

Sophie rested her forehead against Rachel's as they both laughed. "We can continue this later, right?" she said with a smile.

"Oh yes."

"Good, because that bed is far too neat and tidy, it needs christening," Sophie whispered as she leant in for another quick kiss.

"I think we can definitely arrange that, Detective."

The End

ABOUT THE AUTHOR

Claire Highton-Stevenson lives in the UK. She is the author of 'The Cam Thomas Serie: OUT, Next and YES. As well as the highly acclaimed The Promise, and Escape & Freedom.

A keen photographer, traveler and football fan. Claire can often be found brunching with friends in her hometown. She is married. Her wife and herself have a blended family of two cats and two dogs.

If you enjoyed this book, or any other of Claire's books, then please consider leaving a review.

Many thanks!

UK Readers

https://www.amazon.co.uk/default/e/B074G45R1C

US Readers

https://www.amazon.com/Claire-Highton-Stevenson/e/B074G45R1C

French Readers

https://www.amazon.fr/l/B074G45R1C

German Readers

https://www.amazon.de/Claire-Highton-Stevenson/e/B074G45R1C

Australian Readers

https://www.amazon.com.au/s?k=Claire+Highton-Stevenson

If you want to know more about Claire, you can follow her on Social media.

Facebook: https://www.facebook.com/ItsClaStevWriter/

Twitter: https://twitter.com/ClaStevOfficial

Instagram: https://www.instagram.com/itsclastevofficial/

Tumblr: https://www.tumblr.com/blog/itsclastevofficial

Blog: https://wordpress.com/view/itsclastevofficialblog.com

Website: http://www.itsclastevofficial.co.uk

For the chance to win prizes, get exclusive updates on new releases, free stories, and much more, why not sign up to Claire's monthly newsletter?

Subscribe here: http://bit.ly/2OA0WdF

MEET AUTHOR MICHELLE ARNOLD
READ ON FOR A PREVIEW OF A WORLD OF DEMONS, THE 4TH BOOK IN THE DETECTIVE AMY SADLER SERIES

When Michelle Arnold was nine, she bound some of her short stories together into a collection, drew pictures for the cover, and wrote a blurb for the back of the "book" describing herself as though she were a well-known author. She is very excited to now be writing blurbs for the backs of real books that people actually read!

Her published novels include *After Raya, The World The Way It Should Be,* and the first three Detective Amy Sadler books, *Out of the Shadows, Beloved Wife, and With Child.* She has a fourth Amy Sadler book planned.

Ms. Arnold lives in Illinois with her cat, Lily Belle.

For more information, visit:

Facebook.com/MichelleArnoldbooks
https://www.amazon.com/Michelle-Arnold/e/B06XJQ9PWX
twitter.com/Berry2120
Instagram.com/michellearnoldauthor

Prologue

She could hear him coming.

Instinctively, she pulled the thin blanket over her naked body, although she knew it would provide no protection. Her ankle strained against the handcuff that chained her to the metal bedframe, and she could feel the bruise that had formed there.

Her whole body ached. He had broken her right wrist, and she tried her best not to move it, but she would forget sometimes in her drugged stupor. Everything was bruised, and she tried not to think about the painful cuts on her chest, the tally marks he cut into her each time he used her body for his pleasure. They were her best clue as to how long she might have been here. The injections knocked her out for a while, confused her, made her uncertain how much time had passed. How many days had she been away from Amy, undergoing this torture? Amy had to be going crazy looking for her. Lira told herself over and over that Amy would find her, that she couldn't possibly not find her. She tried not to think of the women before her, women Amy had done everything in her power to find. Three women had been in this room before Lira, and none of them had made it out alive.

She glanced desperately around the room, as if there might be some way out that she hadn't noticed yet, but of course there was nothing. She turned away when he came into the room, curling into a ball and squeezing her eyes shut as if she could make him disappear. As always, he pulled the blanket back and stood over her, breathing loudly. She wanted him to die. Lira was a peaceful person, but she thought she could kill him herself, if only she had a weapon. She hated him.

He stroked her face, and she jerked away with a sound of protest.

"I need you to take these pills," he told her. "I need you to sleep longer this time, but when you wake up, I'll have a surprise for you."

Her eyes opened. He rarely spoke to her, had ignored her even when she had spoken to him. He had never mentioned doing something for her. She couldn't imagine it would be something she would actually like.

"I'm not taking any pills," she said softly.

"You need them so I can get you the surprise."

"I don't want it."

"Yes you do. Come on, it's just a few pills. I brought you water."

"No."

"Fine, have it your way." He grabbed her face in his strong hand and forced the pills into her mouth. She scratched savagely at his face with her one good hand, but he had two good hands, and he held her mouth shut until she finally swallowed.

"You won't be fighting like that much longer," he whispered as she began to lose consciousness. "Not when I bring you Amy."

Her eyes widened, and she tried to fight the anesthetic, to claw her way back to alertness. He couldn't bring Amy. She wanted her more than anything in the world, but not here. He would hurt her too. But the drug took over, and soon she was back to oblivion.

When she woke up, she wasn't in the room anymore. She was in a hospital now, and Amy was there, unhurt. He had brought Amy to her just like he said, but she had overpowered him and killed him with his own gun. The nightmare was over.

***

Lira woke again, this time at home. She struggled to catch her breath. She always had dreams about her abduction at this time of year, even almost four years later. It was March, which meant the anniversary was coming. She did her best to ground herself in the present. She was in her own bed, with Amy, who was now her wife, at her side. On her other side was a bassinet, in which their baby girl Ruby was sound asleep. Lira sat up and gazed at the sleeping baby for a few minutes, listening to her slow breathing. Ruby was still innocent, completely unaware of the horrors the world held. Lira hoped to keep her this innocent as long as possible.

Finally she lay back down, her own breathing back to normal. She snuggled up to her wife, who muttered something in her sleep and instinctively wrapped her arms around her. Lira knew she was safe here. Nothing could possibly hurt her in Amy's arms. The dream was gone now, the horrors of not quite four years ago behind her.

She wondered sometimes, though, if it was possible to ever really put something like that behind you.

Chapter 1

"Have your cameras ready. We don't know how fast she's going to tear this thing up," Becky said.

Lira hastily grabbed her DSLR camera as Becky set a round cake on the highchair in front of Ruby. Amy stepped forward and carefully lit the big candle in the shape of the number one. Becky, Amy's mother, had made a lovely little round cake, with sky blue icing providing the background for colorful spring flowers. There was a matching sheet cake for the adults, but Becky had insisted that Ruby had to have her very own cake.

Ruby reached a chubby little hand towards the flame, but Amy quickly caught it with a firm "No."

"Blow out the candle!" Becky encouraged her as Lira took picture after picture. Her little daughter looked so perfect just then. Her hair was a mass of dark, wild curls just like Amy's, her eyes perfectly green (like Lira's, although she really got it from the sperm donor), her cheeks rosy. She was wearing her special first birthday outfit: a dress with a ruffled pink skirt and a birthday cake embroidered on the chest, and a matching sweater with differently colored balloons on it. Over that she wore a bib with a big number 1, and on her head was an elaborate birthday crown that also bore a glittery 1. Her Amish-made high chair was decorated with little pennants spelling out the word "one."

Ruby made several earnest attempts at blowing out her candle, but she hadn't quite mastered the art of blowing yet. Instead she just blew raspberries in the general direction of the flame, getting little drops of spit all over the top of the cake. Finally Amy leaned down and blew the candle out for her before declaring, "You did it!"

"Yaaaay!" Ruby agreed, clapping her little hands. Then she stuck one of her hands directly into the cake.

"Oh," said Lira. "Ruby, I have a fork for you." She turned to the table, looking for the little fork, but Amy stopped her.

"It's her first birthday," said Amy. "Let her make a mess."

Lira looked around and saw it was already too late to stop her. Ruby now had both hands deeply embedded in the cake, a look of rapture on her small face. She lifted one hand to her mouth and took an enormous bite of chocolate cake, smearing much of it on her face in the process. "Yum yum yum," she chanted, reaching for more. Her crown slid off her head and she reached up to touch the spot where it had been, smearing a line of blue icing through her curls. Lira laughed and cringed at the same time.

"I think it's going to take both of us to get her clean after this," she said to Amy. It often did anyway. Ruby didn't mind getting in the water for the sake of splashing, but she wasn't a huge fan of actually being washed.

"Yeah," Amy agreed. "But at least she's having fun."

She definitely was. Lira sighed happily as she watched her little girl gleefully attacking the cake. She had been a mother now for an entire year. Where had the time gone? It seemed like she had only just held that tiny, wriggling body in her arms for the very first time. Now Ruby had tripled in size, was walking and climbing and getting into everything, and she seemed to learn new words each day. She didn't have much time for being held anymore. She already wanted to exert her independence, to spend her time exploring and figuring out how things worked (and how they tasted. Absolutely everything she found went into her mouth). But when she was sleepy, Lira could hold her as long as she wanted, and she felt a sort of peace when Ruby was in her arms that she'd never experienced before. She didn't think she would ever get enough of it.

By the time Ruby was done with her cake, it was smeared all over the high chair, her clothes, her face, her hair, and somehow even her feet. As a grand finale, she pushed the platter onto the floor and started struggling in her seat, yelling "Dow! Dow!"

"Hold on, we have to get you cleaned up first!" said Lira, rushing to get a dishrag. Amy, knowing how tricky this part was, grabbed a rag as well, and they both tackled the problem at once.

While Lira fought to wipe the cake off the struggling toddler's face and hands, Amy tried to get what she could cleaned off her dress and feet. Finally they had her as clean as she was going to get under the circumstances, so Lira removed her bib, unfastened her from the chair, and lifted her out. "There, you can play now," she said, planting a quick kiss on her daughter's head (she had to sneak affection in wherever she could) before setting her down on the floor. Ruby immediately ran to her favorite present: a little ride-on car she could push with her feet. She hopped on and took off through the house, people hastily moving out of her way.

"Well, she's definitely enjoying her birthday," Amy remarked, watching her daughter proudly.

"Yes," agreed Lira. "I think she's going to find a way to get icing all over the house, though."

"That's okay. We're moving out soon anyway," Amy joked. They had, only a few days before, made an offer on a big, beautiful Prairie-style house near the river. Lira was sad about leaving her beloved bungalow, which she had purchased when she was still single, but she loved the new house, and she thought it would be good to have a house that she and Amy decorated together, one that would be *theirs* instead of *hers*. The new house was also a better place for raising children, with a huge yard and four large bedrooms.

"Oh, I can't wait to see the new house in person," said Genevieve, Lira's mother (well, the woman who had raised her, whom she thought of as her mother). "It just looked so gorgeous in the pictures. I think Ruby will love growing up there." Genevieve, a bestselling writer, had recently moved into a stately brick house in an affluent community near Brookwood, which she'd purchased last year after finishing her prison sentence for kidnapping Lira at birth.

"It *is* a nice house, but I'm sad you won't be as close to my house," lamented Becky.

"It's a ten-minute drive, I think you'll live," Amy told her.

The doorbell rang, and Lira hurried to answer it.

"Hey," said Luis, Amy's partner in the Homicide Unit at the Brookwood Police Department. He was holding a present in his hands while his wife Stella stood next to him with their 22-month-old son, Miguel. "Sorry we're late. I got called to a crime scene."

"It's quite all right. I assume Clarissa was there?" Lira and Amy had both made sure they would not be on call this weekend so they could devote themselves entirely to celebrating Ruby's birthday. That meant Lira's fellow forensic pathologist, Clarissa Hill, had to be the one to inspect any dead bodies that turned up.

"Yeah, but she should be on her way here soon. It was kind of gruesome. A woman tied to a tree in the woods, no clothes on. Just about the worst kind of case, except for, you know, kids."

"We can discuss the case when I do the autopsy on Monday," Lira told him firmly. "We're not talking about murder on my daughter's birthday."

"I absolutely agree," said Stella. "So where is the birthday girl?"

"Um…" Lira looked around and located Ruby in the living room, where she was "mowing" the rug with a new wooden push toy that vaguely resembled a lawn mower. She had abandoned her car, which her eight-year-old cousin Nelson was now taking for a spin, even though it was a bit small for him. "There she is. Ruby, Luis and Stella are here! And Miguel!"

Stella put Miguel down, and he immediately ran for the ride-on car, which Nelson gamely gave up for him.

Lira paused for a moment to watch from the doorway. Ruby was enjoying being the center of attention with her noisy extended family all around her: mothers, grandmothers, her aunt and uncles, cousins, friends. Even their golden retriever, Henry, and Himalayan cat, Clea, were in the middle of the action. Lira smiled, feeling pleased that she had brought a child into such a wonderful family.

And, if all went well, they would soon be bringing another child into the family.

***

"I was so busy getting ready for the party, I forgot to make sure you took your prenatal vitamins this morning," Lira said to Amy, turning off the water for Ruby's bath.

"I took them. I don't *always* need you to remind me." Amy pulled Ruby's icing-covered outfit off and plunked the wiggly toddler into the tub.

"Good." Lira put Ruby's toy boat in the water, and Ruby immediately began pushing it around. "So, just ten days left until we do embryo transfer number one." Lira had gotten pregnant with Ruby, Amy's biological child, through IVF, and now it was Amy's turn to do the same with one of Lira's embryos.

"Yeah. I am so ready to carry your baby." Amy gave Lira as a quick kiss as she reached for a washcloth and began scrubbing Ruby, who had managed to get cake even *under* her clothing.

"I can't wait to see you pregnant, although I'm also a little nervous. We have our hands full already with just one. What if we can't handle two?"

"We'll manage. If we were five years younger I'd say wait another year, but we're both pushing forty now. We don't have time to wait. And you don't want Ruby to be an only child, and I want a kid with Lira DNA. So we're going to do this, and we will rise to the challenge, because we've managed so much worse."

"You're right," said Lira, gently pouring warm water over Ruby's icing-streaked hair. "We should be able to handle anything by now. And you want a little brother or sister, don't you, Ruby?"

Ruby looked at her uncertainly. "Bo," she said, holding up her boat.

"Yes, that is a boat," Lira agreed, pleased with how quickly her daughter's vocabulary was expanding. She was already well ahead of most twelve-month-olds.

"I'm not sure what the message is there," Amy chuckled.

"Maybe that she'd rather have a boat than a sibling?" Lira laughed. "Okay, I need to wash her hair. Are you ready?"

"I've got this." Amy picked up a little bubble kit Ruby had gotten for her birthday. "Hey, Ruby. Watch this!" She began blowing bubbles in Ruby's direction.

"Oooo!" exclaimed Ruby, reaching for the bubbles while Lira hastily squeezed baby shampoo onto her head and began working it through unruly curls.

"You popped it!" said Amy. "Look, here come some more." She blew more bubbles, and Ruby eagerly popped them as Lira made sure she got out every last bit of icing.

"Pop!" Ruby yelled excitedly.

"Pop! That's right!" Amy encouraged her, blowing more bubbles. "You pick up fast!"

"She's so smart," Lira murmured contentedly, rinsing the shampoo back out of Ruby's hair. This took at least as much concentration as making an incision during an autopsy. One false move, on her part or Ruby's, and there would be shampoo in the baby's eyes. At least corpses didn't move. "There," Lira announced triumphantly when all the suds were gone. "We have a clean baby!"

"All right! Good job, Doctor!" Amy high-fived her.

"We make an excellent team," Lira said, grinning. She grabbed a hooded towel and lifted Ruby out of the tub.

"*Pop!*" Ruby yelled, pointing at the bubble wand in Amy's hand. Amy resumed blowing bubbles while Lira dried Ruby off.

"I'm sort of dreading going to work Monday and doing the autopsy on that victim Luis was talking about. Clarissa's going to be off that day, so it'll fall on me."

Amy looked up. "Yeah, I heard him. It sounds like a rough one."

Lira nodded, wrestling Ruby into a clean diaper and pajamas while the toddler continued popping bubbles. "She was found nude, so there's a good chance..." She trailed off, knowing Amy got the point and not wanting to say the words in front of Ruby. "I always find those cases a bit triggering. I try to look at it professionally, the way I used to, but I can't anymore. It throws me off for the rest of the day."

"You could always recuse yourself from the autopsy. It can wait until Clarissa's back."

"I could, but then I think I'd feel even worse. The thing is, it happens, much too often, and I can't change that by avoiding these cases. I *can* help put away the people who do it, though."

"That's always the most satisfying part."

"Yes. And I think the feeling I get when I know I've helped prevent the perpetrator from doing the same thing to anyone else outweighs the bad feeling I get from thinking about the case."

"That's a good way of looking at it. I think there's a sort of poetic justice to you helping to bring down, you know, that kind of bad guy. It's my favorite kind of bad guy to get off the street, which is why I don't mind working those cases, even if it is unsettling."

"Mommy!" whined Ruby, her arms up. Lira picked her up and carried her into the nursery, settling into the glider to breastfeed her.

"Do you thinking we did the right thing, bringing her into a world where *that* sort of thing happens?" Lira asked softly, cradling Ruby in her arms.

"Well." Amy perched on the arm of the glider, putting one arm around Lira while running her fingers through Ruby's damp curls. "We also brought her into a world where *this* sort of thing happens."

Printed in Great Britain
by Amazon

84146847R00173